THE FRAME!

He stared at the blade, and the dizziness vanished and a cold terror washed over him. He opened his taut, frozen fingers and let the knife slip down to the rug. It quivered and was still. Suddenly he rose up from the chair and went over to her, and as he came to her side, he stopped stock-still and opened his lips in a silent scream.

He kept staring down at the deep wound.

"Donna," he whispered.

She was dead.

———————

"A spare, serpentine tale
told by an old master of suspense."
Richard Peck, Author of
Are You in the House Alone?

"THE PIGEON by Jay Bennett
is a slick, rapid-fire
mystery. . . . Another spellbinder."
The Detroit News

"Jay Bennett deftly
draws readers into a web of terror."
School Library Journal

Other Avon Flare Books by
Jay Bennett

THE KILLING TREE

THE
PIGEON

JAY BENNETT

AN AVON FLARE BOOK

AVON BOOKS
A division of
The Hearst Corporation
959 Eighth Avenue
New York, New York 10019

The Methuen, Inc. edition contains the following Library
of Congress Cataloging in Publication Data:

Bennett, Jay.
  The pigeon.

SUMMARY: Responding to his former girlfriend's
plea for help, 17-year-old Brian goes to her
Greenwich Village apartment only to find her dead
and himself framed for her murder. He vows to
find her killers and the reason for her death.
  [1. Terrorism—Fiction. 2. Mystery and
detective stories. 3. New York (City)—Fiction]
I. Title.
PZ7.B4399Pi   [Fic]

First Flare Printing, August, 1981

FLARE trademark application is pending before
the U.S. Patent and Trademark Office.

Printed in the U.S.A.

10 9 8 7 6 5 4 3 2

For Phyllis

1

He was sitting in the upstairs room, just sitting there and looking out through the window at the tree and the way the sun was beginning to fade on its leaves, when he heard the sound of the phone and then his mother's voice calling up to him.

"It's for you, Brian."

"Thanks," he shouted down.

Then he picked up the phone still looking out at the old, darkening tree and thinking how he used to climb it when he was much younger. . . .

"Hello?"

"Brian?"

It was Donna.

"Yes?"

He felt a tremor go through him.

"Brian, can I see you tonight?"

He was still looking at the tree, but now he was concentrating upon her voice. It was quiet and low as usual but there was an urgency to it.

The house became silent about him.

"Well, I . . ." he hesitated.

Silent and hollow. Nobody in it but the voice on the phone.

"Please, Brian."

And he said to himself it's over six weeks since we spoke to each other. Six weeks and two days since we had that argument over the weirdo crowd she was running around with.

"Brian?"

And he thought now there was fear in her voice.

"Will you come?"

This was so unlike her.

"Okay," he said. "I'll be there."

"Thanks," she said, and he thought she was about to cry.

"Donna, I'll take the eight o'clock bus in. Figure an hour and a quarter from then, and I'll be ringing your bell."

"I'll wait for you, Brian."

The voice was quiet and low and controlled now.

"An hour and a quarter."

There was a pause. He waited for her to speak again. He could almost see her sitting at the phone, her face tight and controlled but her hands trembling.

He was sure her hands were trembling.

"You'll start now, Brian?" she said suddenly.

"It's too early yet for the eight o'clock bus, Donna."

"Oh. That's right."

There was a silence. And then he heard her voice again. Sudden and lonely.

"You'll start right away, Brian?"

"Donna," he said gently. "Donna, I told you it's too . . ."

"That's right," she cut in. "It's too early. It's always too early or it's always too late, isn't it?"

"What do you mean?"

"Oh, nothing. Nothing."

And again he thought she was about to cry.

"Donna."

"You won't miss the bus, will you, Brian?"

"I won't. Donna, what is . . . ?"

"You're sure now?"

"I'll make it, Donna."

And he was about to say, What's wrong, Donna? What is frightening you? Who is it? But then he heard the click and he put the receiver slowly back onto its hook, and then he sat there a long time thinking of her.

Long, long thoughts.

"Brian?"

He slowly turned and saw his mother standing hesitant in the narrow doorway of the small room.

"Yes?"

Her shadow wavered over one of the yellow walls and then onto the sloping white ceiling. Wavered and was still.

"Was that Donna?"

He didn't answer.

She was a tall and slender woman, almost as tall as Brian, and her face was still young and attractive. She was forty-five, and he was just past seventeen.

"Was it, Brian?"

"You know it was," he said, his grey eyes steady upon her.

She flinched and looked past him to the schoolbooks opened out on his desk. The study notes for his upcoming finals. He was to graduate from Elton High in two months.

Donna had already graduated and was now in New York at NYU.

"Are you going to see her tonight?"

"I guess so."

"Then maybe you won't be back?"

"Maybe not tonight. I'll take a few books with me. I might stay over at her place."

He had his mother's clear, straight features. Her dark shining hair and her high cheekbones. There was nothing of his father in him, nothing of that stocky, rugged man she had divorced eight years ago. Except for the cool grey eyes. The very eyes that had originally attracted her to the man.

"Brian."

Outside, the light was moving away from the house and the trees and the smooth, silent lawn.

The clean sidewalk with its long line of hedges was empty and still, waiting for the night to sweep in.

"Yes?"

"Why don't you stay home?"

He shook his head gently. "Can't."

She came farther into the room and now he saw the pallor on her face.

"You'll study a bit more and then we'll drive out to one of the late movies. I haven't any date tonight so we can spend some time together."

"No, Mom. I'm sorry. Some other time."

"There's a good one at the Paramus Mall. A Jane Fonda and . . . and . . . an. . . ." Her voice trailed away into a defeated silence.

"Donna seems to need me," he said.

"Needs you?"

"Uh-huh."

"Why? What's wrong?"

"I don't know. I'll find out when I speak to her."

"Your finals are coming up."

"I know, Mom," he said, and a weary tone came into his voice.

"Your finals," she said again and was silent.

But it's not my finals at all, Mother. Not that at all, he thought. It's Donna. You never liked her. In fact, you feared her. As you do now.

"Brian."

"Well?"

She placed her hand on his shoulder. He sat there looking up at her.

"Please stay home."

"Why?"

"I—I have a feeling."

"What do you mean?"

Outside a car passed down the street and then all was still again. The air in the room was close and warm.

10

He saw little beads of perspiration on his mother's forehead. Little gleaming beads. She barely moved her lips when she spoke.

"I just—can't explain."

His grey eyes bored into her. "Try."

"It—it's an intuition."

"A mother's intuition?"

"You're laughing at me."

He shook his head sombrely. "I'm not. Really I'm not."

She breathed in deeply.

"All right. A mother's intuition."

"That something will happen to me?"

"Yes."

"What? For example?"

"I—I don't know."

She waited for him to speak, but he said nothing. He felt her hand cold on his shoulder. Cold and damp. He saw the fear in her eyes.

"Don't go," she said.

Then he watched her turn, and then he heard her go down the stairs—slow, measured steps. The room was quiet again. Her shadow was no longer there.

He sat looking at the tree, and he remembered standing under it with Donna. He remembered that.

Suddenly the night fell and the tree was dark.

2

He sat in the darkness of the eight o'clock bus, and
then somewhere in the middle of the run to the city
somebody started to play a guitar softly; it came from
the back of the bus, from a huddled figure in the back
of the bus. Brian listened to the low melody, and then
he closed his eyes and thought of Donna.

He saw her again, his arm about her as they walked
under the bare trees, with the twilight of a winter's
day just falling.

We were so close to each other, he said to himself.
Always that way. And then this stupid breakup.

He opened his eyes and looked out through the
window at the passing lights, the blots of darkness,
and he listened to the melody floating through the bus.

What is she frightened of?

What is it, Donna?

If I could only see her now. This moment. And he
turned in his seat almost expecting to see her sitting
next to him, a curious smile on her face.

Tears hovering in her large, brown eyes.

We should never have quarreled, Brian. Never.
How could you stand being away from me all these

weeks without hearing my voice or seeing my face?

I couldn't. I suffered, Brian. I suffered greatly.

But we're both stubborn idiots, aren't we? We get our backs up and there's no moving us, is there?

Brian?

He looked at the empty seat next to him, and his lips tightened in a straight, painful line.

What fools we are, he thought bitterly. *We make our own damned troubles. We never know when we're ahead of the game.*

What is frightening you, Donna?

What is it?

And suddenly, softly, the low, ghostly voice of the huddled guitar player opened into the night and these strange and haunting words were carried down the rows to Brian.

> Weep for Daddy-O
> O weep for Daddy-O
> You die once
> You die twice
> Just ain't no difference
> 'Cause dying once is enough
> 'Cause dying once is forever

The last words were whispered in a foggy voice, and then they faded away and the bus went on into the heavy darkness of the night.

The words and the melody stayed with him as he walked through the Port Authority Bus Terminal and then down into the subway.

Only when he got out at the Christopher Street station did the haunting words and the slow melody leave him.

Only then.

But somehow, even though the May night was warm and the Greenwich Village streets bright and bustling, he felt within him a chill starting to settle.

13

3

He came to her street—it really was an alley—a quiet, placid alley with old brownstones and spaced plane trees. Small shadowy trees with glistening leaves. He walked slowly down the alley, passing from splash of lamplight into darkness and then again into splash of lamplight. He walked till he came to the alley's winding end, to an old narrow tenement that had recently been renovated and divided into small studio apartments.

It had a stone stoop of four steps.

A fellow sat on the top step, sat leaning against the black iron railing. He smoked a cigarette and looked lazily out across the street into the night. Brian glanced at him and went up the steps, his hand on the black iron railing, the streetlamp glowing down on his tall, lean figure, shining white on his sneakers.

"Nice night," the fellow said.

Brian paused and looked down at the seated man.

"Yes," he said, and didn't know why he was lingering.

The fellow smiled. He had long blond hair that went to his shoulders and a round face with gentle

14

blue eyes. He wore a fringed deerskin jacket and tooled leather boots. His cowboy hat lay at his side.

He was in his early twenties, Brian thought, and turned to go into the house where Donna was waiting for him.

"Goin' to get better as it goes along," the fellow said in a low, easy voice.

Brian stood there, almost held to the spot. The fellow lifted the cigarette to his lips with a slow motion, took a deep drag and then exhaled. Brian saw a large gold ring on his middle finger. The ring was shaped into the figure of a snake, and the head had two tiny diamonds that glittered through the wavering blue smoke.

"Better and better."

The ringed hand threw the cigarette out into the empty street. It glowed, a pinpoint of fierce light, and then went out.

"Goin' to have a warm spring and a hot summer."

"Looks like it," Brian said.

The fellow nodded. "That's what my daddy always said on a night like this. Name's Curley."

Brian hesitated and again turned to go, but he heard himself speaking.

"Brian."

"Live around here?"

Brian shook his head, and as he did, the weird image of the Ancient Mariner floated through his mind.

"Just visiting," Brian said.

"Come from New York, Brian?"

"Used to live here a while," Brian said. "I live in Jersey now."

It was as if this fellow had stopped him, like the Ancient Mariner had stopped the wedding guest, and he, Brian, had to stand there and talk to him.

"Just across the river?"

"A little farther in."

It was something powerful and magnetic in the man. He held you there. Where you were. Held you

15

there, while within you had an uncomfortable and chilling feeling.

"I come from Ohio. No place like New York."

"It's interesting."

Curley's eyes flashed. "More than interesting, friend. It's fascinating, man. Fascinating."

"Okay with me if you find it that way," Brian said.

"That's how I find it."

Curley picked his hat up and delicately put it on his head. He shaped the brim, the ringed hand glowing as it caught the flare of the lamplight.

"How long did you live in New York, Brian?"

"Just a year," Brian said.

"And you didn't come to love it?"

"No," Brian said.

Curley rose to his feet. He was about Brian's height. He was broad-shouldered and powerfully built.

"Fascinating town," he said. "I'll never leave it."

"I guess you won't," Brian said. Suddenly he was angry at himself for staying and talking with the man.

"Good talking to you, Brian."

"Same," Brian said.

"I like you," Curley smiled. "I see someone and I know right off if I'm goin' to like or hate the man. And I can hate."

Brian didn't say anything.

"You've got a friend," Curley said.

Brian watched the fellow go down the steps and walk up the alley and slowly disappear into the night.

But the last image in his mind was not the figure of the cowboy with its fringed jacket and broad-brimmed hat. . . .

It was the glittering eyes of the ring.

Glittering through the wavering blue smoke.

4

Brian stood on the stone stoop, gazing down the alley at the splash of lights and the still leaves of the trees glistening in the intervening darkness. A cowboy from Ohio, he thought to himself. Make a good title for a bizarre movie. Then he turned away, released from the man, but he realized that the cold chill was still deep within him.

He opened the glass front door of the building and stood in a small vestibule. He went over to the tenants' panel and looked for her name—Donna Madison—and for an instant he couldn't find it and suddenly the fear that was deep within him began to filter upward.

His hands trembled as he found her name and pressed the black button next to it. He waited for the buzzer to sound, the buzzer that would open the door for him. But there was silence.

Donna, he whispered.

He pressed the button again, leaned forward and put his lips to the mouthpiece.

"Donna?"

Still no answering buzzer. He found himself standing there in the vestibule, almost closed in, and wanting to hear her voice.

He pressed the button again and then tried the door. But the door wouldn't open.

"Donna. It's Brian," he called into the mouthpiece.

He began to wonder if she was in the apartment. He desperately pressed the button, this time a long time, and then the buzzing began, fierce and insistent.

He swung away from the panel and sharply turned the knob of the door and went into the hallway. He stood there alone, and the words of his mother came back to him.

Don't go, Brian.

He went slowly up a flight of carpeted stairs.

The house was silent. He heard the muffled laugh of a woman's voice, the shrill cry of a child in another perspective, and then the silence flooded in again.

But when he came to the third floor landing, the sound of music drifted down to him, a hazy sound. It was loud and yet it seemed to come from behind a closed door. He went up the last flight, listening to the music, and he could barely make out a Kenny Rogers song . . .

The voice, plaintive and hovering . . .

When he came to the fourth and top floor of the building, he paused and leaned against the polished wood balustrade.

The music was coming from Donna's apartment.

Donna, he whispered to himself.

His grey eyes searched the dim hallway for her. He had expected to see her standing at the doorway of her apartment, waiting for him.

Donna.

Brian.

I'm here, Donna. As soon as I could get here. What's wrong?

I'll tell you inside.

It's so good to see you again, Donna.

It's so good to see you again, Brian.

Let's never quarrel again.

Never, Brian. Never again. I promise you that.

But there was no one.

His hand tightened over the two textbooks he was carrying. Then he went down the hallway to her closed door.

He could now hear clearly the Kenny Rogers vocal and the backup music, and he wondered why she was playing it so loud.

Donna always liked her music soft, low and even. No matter what kind it was, even hard rock. She would sit on the floor against a chair, kick off her shoes, and let her head go back, her head with its sweep of long, soft brown hair, and she would listen, and then her deep brown eyes would become intense and absorbed.

The wild cynical look that was ever in their depths —the look that said to hell with this absurd world, it's all a crock—now gone from them. And it was in these precious, vagrant moments that he always felt closest to her, closest to what he knew was the true Donna.

He rang the bell and waited.

"Donna?"

He rang the bell again, this time hard and long.

"Donna."

But no one came to the door.

"It's Brian. What the hell's the matter?"

His voice sounded high and harsh against a swelling chord of music. He hit the door twice with his fist, and then he put his hand to the doorknob and turned it violently. The door opened, smoothly and easily.

He stepped into the apartment. The room was in utter darkness. The blinds of the windows were drawn tight.

The only light came from the hallway, filtering into the apartment. A cold, wavering ray.

He stepped farther into the darkness and bumped into an overturned chair and almost fell over it to the floor.

"Where are you?" he called out.

And now there was fear and concern in his voice. One of the blinds moved in the night breeze, and a long, thin sliver of light came into the room. He sensed that someone was there with him, standing silent and alone. He felt a cold sweat break out all over his body. His big hands began to tremble, and he almost dropped the books.

"Donna, for Christ. . . ."

Suddenly the door slammed shut behind him. He heard the sound, loud and savage, against the poignant music.

Brian froze and then turned sharply around, and as he did, he saw the vague outlines of a figure and an arm raised high.

The faint gleam of a gun barrel.

And before he could even cry out in terror, he felt a jarring thud on his head. The books fell from his hand like stones. Then his legs began to crumple under him, and he sank to the floor.

The darkness and the music swept over him.

5

It was the pungent smell of whiskey that made him open his eyes. And it came from his wet shirt. His left hand moved cautiously, tentatively over it, felt the wetness, and he slowly realized that someone had poured whiskey over him.

He turned his head, felt it throb, and looked about him.

One of the lamps was lit. The other lamp lay shattered on the rug, its pushed over end table next to it. He saw an overturned armchair in the far shadows of the room, close to one of the grey walls, and then nearer to him an empty whiskey bottle gleamed, and then the cold shine of two glasses lying on the rug.

It came to him that the music had been turned off.

His gaze slowly, painfully circled to the couch, and he saw Donna lying on it. She was wearing grey slacks and a thin grey sweater. Her shoes were on the floor beside her. As if she had just kicked them off.

One of her arms was spread out, her hand just reaching over the end of the couch. He lay on the floor, lazily noting the grace of the slender, tapering fingers.

She was sleeping.

He got slowly to his feet, a fierce, throbbing pain in his head. There was something wrong with his right hand, and yet he didn't look down to see what it was. All of his being was now concentrated upon Donna.

Was she sleeping?

Yes, yes, of course, of course.

I can even see how lightly she is breathing. Her face so pale and calm. Her hair about her . . . shimmering in the lamplight. . . .

He stood there swaying and then he heard from out in the hallway the sound of someone walking slow, measured steps. He listened, all the time looking at Donna, and then the sound drifted away and dimmed out on the staircase.

The house was still again.

He walked a few steps to her and suddenly felt very dizzy. The room began to swirl about him. He grabbed one of the chairs with his left hand and set it straight and sank down upon it.

And it was then, only then, that he saw what was wrong with his right hand. He was carrying a long-bladed knife in its grip.

He stared at the blade, and the dizziness vanished and a cold terror washed over him. He opened his taut, frozen fingers and let the knife slip down to the rug. It quivered and was still. Suddenly he rose up from the chair and went over to her, and as he came to her side, he stopped stock-still and opened his lips in a silent scream.

He kept staring down at the deep wound.

"Donna," he whispered.

She was dead.

6

He sat on the rug at her side, stroking her long, soft brown hair and pressing her limp hand to his lips and crying in a low, agonized voice, crying her name again and again in a broken litany.

And it was then that the phone rang.

He let it ring, and then it stopped. And then it immediately started up again, a cold, insistent ringing, and then it stopped.

And then it started again.

As if calling to him.

Calling to him to come and answer.

He went over to it and picked up the receiver and said nothing. Just stood there waiting, holding the receiver to his ear, a distant, lost look in his grey eyes. His face was white and drawn, the tears still glistening on his lean cheeks.

His body was taut and trembling.

Then he heard the voice.

"Brian Cawley?"

He had never heard that voice before.

"Get out of the apartment. Get out as fast as you can."

"What?"

The word was torn out of him.

"You're being set up."

The man's voice was low and urgent.

"What do you mean?"

"You're being set up. You're being made a pigeon. Get out and run for your life. Listen to me. There's nothing you can do for her now."

"Who are you?"

The voice became harsh.

"What the hell does it matter? Get out. You're wasting time. You haven't got a chance, pigeon. They'll lock you up for murder."

"Murder?"

"For her murder."

Brian's hand tightened over the receiver till the knuckles showed white. His lips began to tremble.

"Donna's?"

"Donna's," the voice said, like an echo.

He felt the dizziness break over him again. The voice seemed to come to him from a distance. A long and hazy distance.

"She's dead, my friend."

"No," Brian whispered.

"Dead. And you're caught in a trap."

He stood there in a humming silence and waited for the man to speak again. It seemed to be an eternity, and yet it was only a matter of a few seconds.

"A setup, Brian. You smell from whiskey. It's all over you. The chairs overturned. Lamp and glasses over the floor. The knife in your hand. That's how the police are supposed to find you."

You know it all, Brian thought bitterly. As if you were standing here in this room. Standing at my side.

The voice went on relentlessly.

"They stuck a knife in your hand. Closed your fingers tightly over the handle. Your prints are now on it."

Brian stared down at the knife. It lay where he had

dropped it. Lay glinting in the grey shadows of the fallen chair.

"You got drunk. You quarreled with her. You killed her."

"Shut up," Brian said.

"You killed her. With that knife."

"No," Brian shouted. "No."

"Brian, Brian."

The voice softened. It was a young voice, Brian sensed, of a fellow in his twenties. No more than that.

"I'm only telling you what the police will say."

"The police," Brian murmured and was silent.

"Start running."

Brian stood there, his face hard and grim, and a surge of despair went through him. He looked over to where she lay on the couch as if sleeping. Lay there so quietly and at rest. As if sleeping.

Soon to wake and smile at him.

"Donna," he whispered pleadingly.

And as he did, the wild thought swept through him that she was sleeping. Yes, he said to himself, she is, she is.

Oh, God, please say yes. Say she is.

Please.

Donna, you're sleeping and you'll wake up and speak to me. You will.

But then he heard his own voice speak into the phone. It seemed to come from another being.

"I didn't kill Donna."

"The police will soon be there, Brian. Any minute. Do you hear me?"

"But I . . ."

"They'll grab you and throw away the key."

"I didn't kill her," Brian murmured.

"Try telling them that. They'll throw the book at you. You'll be sent up for twenty-five years. You'll be better off dead."

"I . . . didn't . . . kill . . . her. . . ."

His voice trailed off into silence.

"Get out of the apartment."

"Who killed her?" Brian suddenly asked.

"There is a stairway to the roof. Use it, pigeon. Use it. Now."

"Who killed her?" Brian's voice rose and filled the room. "Why was she killed? Why?"

"Start running, pigeon. For your life."

"Tell me. You know why she was killed. Tell me."

There was a silence and then a click.

7

He had given her a locket on her last birthday. A golden locket with a thin golden chain. And in the locket he had put a little oval picture, his picture.

I will always treasure this, Brian.

It's for you, Donna.

It's so beautiful.

For you, Donna.

It must've cost you a lot.

A little. I saved up from the summer job.

I will always wear it, Brian. To the end of my life.

Just wear it. Till you meet another guy.

To the end of my life, Brian.

And now as he looked down on her face for the last time and saw the locket, he whispered to her, "To the end of your life, Donna. You did. You did."

He put his hand to the chain and tenderly lifted it and the gleaming locket over her calm white face and over her soft brown hair, soft and rippling, and held it in his hand.

It felt warm to his touch. Warm and throbbing. So very alive.

I will always wear it, Donna.

Always, Donna.
To the end of my life.
I swear this to you.

He bent down to kiss her hair, his lips brushed her forehead, and he heard the sound of the sirens. He tensed, and then straightened up; a wild hunted look came onto his face. He listened to the growing, terrifying sound, and then he rushed to the window and pushed aside the blinds and stared down into the dark street.

He saw the first police car and then the other, their lights slashing into the night. Then he heard the slam of the car doors.

Brian turned away from the window, letting the blinds come to with a sharp, grating sound. He stood there an instant, rigid, panic spreading like a flame within him, a hot, searing flame; then he thrust the locket into the side pocket of his jeans and ran to the door. He opened it and stepped out into the dim hallway. He paused and looked frantically around for the stairway and then he saw it, a flight of stone steps that led upward to the roof. He ran to it and climbed the steps, two at a time, till he came to a grey metal door.

There was a snap lock on the door. His sweaty fingers slipped over the round metal knob. He heard the sound of voices rising from below.

"It's the fourth floor."

"Let's go."

He heard the sound of other doors opening in the building, the scatter of voices, and then he jammed open the door and went hurtling out onto the roof. He felt the rush of the warm night air upon him, and he looked up at the dark moonless sky, his face white and taut, and then he bent his head and ran, feeling the gravel spray under his feet. He came to the end of the building and then crossed over the roof of the next one, running hard, his breath in gasps, till he came to a low parapet and he stopped short. Chest heaving.

There was a gap of almost ten feet between the

building upon which Brian stood and the next one. He peered over the parapet and down into the well of darkness below. His body shook with fear.

He heard a far shout from behind him.

"Stay where you are."

He turned involuntarily and saw outlined against the open doorway of Donna's building the dark figure of a policeman. The gleam of the visor, the glitter of the gold buttons and then light shining upon the metal barrel of the gun.

"Don't move. Stay there."

The figure began to step away from the background of light and slowly and surely advance into the darkness.

Advance toward him like a brutal and relentless fate.

Ever closing in on him.

"No," Brian suddenly said. "No."

He climbed onto the brick parapet, stood poised, while his eyes frantically sought the vague outlines of the roof of the other building, and then he took a deep, deep breath, just as he once had when he dove from a great height down into a quarry pool, and he leaped into the night. His body bent forward, his arms reached out, hands clutching the air, reaching, ever reaching for the safety of the other roof, the life-giving safety, yet the hands clutched air, only cold, cold air, and a sinking, sickening sensation coursed through his being, and he began to scream within, I'm falling, falling, I'll never make it, never, Donna, Donna, Donna, why? why? Why, *Donnnnnnnnnnnnnnnnnnnnnn!*

His feet landed on the tar surface of the roof and his body fell forward. He sprawled there, his lips tasting the acrid tar, and then he got to his feet and began to run again, and it was then that he heard the far shouts.

"Stop! Stop!"

"We'll shoot!"

"Stop! Dammit! Stop!"

And then the sound of two shots, like the breaking

of glass, and he felt a soft slap, soft and firm, just above his left elbow, in the hard flesh of the arm, and he knew he had been hit.

"God," he whispered. "God help me. Please."

His arm hung at his side. He wanted to fall forward, fall and lie on the roof, lie there and let the soothing darkness of the night sweep over him.

Darkness and forgetfulness.

But he found himself running, running, his feet pounding the roof of one building and then onto the next one; the shouts were far behind him now, and soon distance blotted out the voices. He ran in a well of silence. The only sounds were the sounds of his feet thudding along and the deep, steady gasp of his breath.

Deep and agonized.

He jumped another gap between roofs and was now on another block. He ran, and on one roof he set a flock of pigeons whirring into the air, their forms dark and quivering against the night. His eyes watched their desperate, panic-stricken flight, and a hopeless, sardonic look came into them.

Pigeons.

He ran, till he came to the top of an old abandoned warehouse that stood at the end of a dismal street. Beyond it was Alder Street, and after that, the waterfront.

Brian knew the building and the empty lot next to it. He had walked past the old warehouse many times with Donna. The old, rusted fire escape had long fallen away from the walls of the sagging structure. Brian turned away from the fire escape and ran to the roof doorway. The door hung crazily on one of its hinges, creaking in the soft wind of the night. From the river he heard the sound of a boat whistle, long and piercing.

Brian shoved the door aside and entered the deserted building. He stopped on the top step and felt his throbbing arm; he groaned softly, and then he descended staircase after staircase, his shadow large on the dusty walls, and all about him was an empty, glooming stillness.

There were dust-covered wooden crates lined up like coffins, row after row, along the cold, stone floors. The air about him was close and clammy. He heard the scurry of rat feet, their nails scraping the cement floor, and an icy fear went through him.

When he got to the ground floor he turned and ran to the back of the building, bumping into crates and knocking them aside in his panic. He found a broken window, large enough to let him through, and he jumped out and onto hard ground.

He paused and caught his breath. His face and body were wet with perspiration. His eyes pierced the night, searching along the length of the empty lot till they found the square bulk that rose two stories high in the night. It was an old movie house that had closed down almost five years ago.

Brian leaned against the wall of the warehouse, the night quiet about him, and now his grey eyes were steady, his breath more even. His panic threaded away from him. He put his hand to the wound and felt the dribbling, warm blood. He knew it was not a deep wound. The bullet had come from too great a distance. It was almost a spent bullet; that's what his father would have said. The father who used to take him hunting and then cleared out of his life. Right after the divorce. And not another word from him. Not a mumbling word. The father he had loved. And still loved.

A spent bullet, Brian. But it's got to come out.

How is the bleeding? Not too bad. Could be a lot worse. You're lucky.

Use your belt. Remember when you cut your leg with your hunting knife? Remember what I did then?

Brian took off his belt and looped it around the arm, above the wound, and then with his teeth tasting the old leather, he made the loop tight.

He sighed out, his mouth open wide.

He leaned back against the wall, and he stood

31

there, swaying and fighting off a sudden surge of weakness and despair. He put his hand to his forehead and then to his cheek.

They were cold and clammy.

You'd better get going, Brian.

He could swear it was his father's voice whispering close to him. He turned for a moment in panic. And then his lips thinned and his lean face tautened. The thoughts and image of his father left him. He moved away from the wall, took a deep breath, and began to run again. He raced across the lot, his feet kicking cans out of the way. His sneaker hit an empty beer bottle, and he almost slipped and fell, but he righted himself and sped on.

A cat darted in front of him and suddenly stopped and backed off, its long black body hunched up, its large eyes pools of fire. Brian came to a sudden halt and stared at the cat. The eyes seemed to burn into him.

The wound in his arm flamed, and he could swear he could hear the drops of blood, tiny drops of blood falling to the ground. In endless rhythm.

"Get out of my way," he suddenly shouted, his voice echoing against the night. The cat turned with a cry and ran off into the darkness; the fire in the eyes was snuffed out.

But the flame in Brian's arm remained, dull and glowing.

"Damn fool," Brian said, and his voice sounded distant and strange to him. "A damn fool thing to do. To shout. You want to tell the cops where you are?"

He turned and ran with a madness till he reached the alley of the movie house, and then he stopped, chest heaving, and searched about him till he saw the outlines of a fire escape. It stood looming above him, like a huge steel skeleton of a prehistoric monster.

He stood there looking at it, and he laughed, a silent, mirthless laugh. And he thought for a flashing instant of the skeleton of a tyrannosaurus he had seen in the Museum of Natural History. He was only ten years old then, and Ellen Fisher, his teacher, had taken the class there.

Ellen Fisher. Who lived just a short distance away in Soho.

He saw her warm, expansive face again, and the memory stayed with him as he went down the alley and came to the fire escape. It was a broad one that led directly to the roof of the building.

"Good," he whispered.

He had worked summers in a theatre, and he knew now where he could go and hide. To get a few hours' rest and try to figure things out.

And then he said to himself bitterly, Damn fool, what is there to figure out? You're a pigeon and Donna, Donna, is dead.

His face was ashen and the dull glow was in his arm as he walked up the fire escape with slow, weary steps. He stopped just before reaching the top, and he felt a surge of weakness and nausea come over him. He wanted to lean over and throw up. His hand gripped the railing with all his remaining strength, and his lips pressed tightly together into a thin line. He stayed that way till the feeling left him.

"Christ," he murmured.

Then he stepped onto the roof and moved across it till he found the side ladder that led down to the inside of the theatre's marquee. And as he paused to peer down into the darkness, he remembered the burst of sunlight, of easy summer sunlight, and he lying on the floor of the Elton Theatre marquee, lying naked, his usher's uniform folded neatly beside him, lying there, eyes closed and letting the sun bake into him. It was his lunch hour and he always went up to the concrete overhang on clear days to sunbathe. No one could see him as he lay there. And he let no one know of his hiding place.

Sometimes he would take up a small iron dumbbell with him, and he would do some exercises to build up his arms.

That was a thousand years ago, he said to himself. In another time.

In another world.

Brian stirred, and then he climbed down the iron ladder, rung by rung, till he reached the bottom. The walls of the marquee rose to about four feet high. Brian made his way through the darkness to one of the walls. He looked out and down into the street.

All was dark and deserted.

"Good," he whispered.

There was a streetlamp at the end of the lonely block. A splash of cold light against the silent dark hulks of buildings.

Brian went to the side wall and peered down into the empty lot. Nothing moved there. He was safe. He had found himself a fortress.

A cave.

He breathed out in silent relief and then sank down against one of the walls of the cave, and it was only then that he realized that there were hot tears on his face and in his eyes.

"Donna," he said.

8

It was the sound of the car that made him open his eyes. Of a car going slowly, slowly, its tires moving over sand and gravel and then a tin can. The clatter of a tin can. He got to his feet and felt a stiffness all over him. He trembled in the night air, and then he moved swiftly over to the wall of the marquee. When he came close to it, he bent down and peered over into the lot. He saw the flashing lights of the police car and then the beam of its searchlight piercing the darkness.

He watched the cold powerful beam as it swept over the huge lot in a relentless arc. The car moving slowly, slowly in a vast silence. He watched it move away from him till it came to the warehouse building. And then the beam moved with its harsh light over the ghostly structure. It focused on the fire escape hanging loose.

Then the beam left the building and turned as the car turned and came back slowly, slowly across the lot till it came closer and closer and began sweeping the dark bulk of the movie house. Brian crouched down on the floor of the marquee, his body tense and shaking. His whole being alert.

They'll never find me.

Never.

They'll give up and go away.

He heard the car stop and then the sound of a car door slamming against the night. And then another slam.

Then silence. Complete silence.

What now?

He bent forward listening, straining, ever straining to catch the slightest sound, and then he heard footsteps on metal. Ascending. Ever ascending.

A cold sweat broke out all over him. His lips quivered, and his eyes became large and staring.

He listened to the two men coming up the broad stairs of the fire escape. Each heavy footstep seemed to get louder and louder, magnified by his terror, till he thought his eardrums would shatter.

There was a sudden, sharp stillness. They had stopped. And now all he heard was the sound of a boat whistle from far off in the river.

Distant and mournful.

And before it faded out he heard the sound of voices, low and penetrating.

"Nothing up here, Ed."

"I guess so."

And he could sense the two figures standing at the beginning of the roof, their searchlights scanning the darkness, their eyes cold and glinting, their guns gripped in their hands.

"Always good to take a look."

"He's out of the area by now. Maybe even out of the city."

"He's got a bullet in him. I know I hit him. I saw his arm go up."

The voices had come closer. They were now halfway across the roof.

"He'll have to take care of it sooner or later. He'll

36

be picked up at one of the hospital emergency rooms."

"Or maybe he'll try a doctor."

"I don't think so."

Then there was a silence, and he thought they had turned to go. He listened with held breath for the sound of their footsteps once more on the fire escape.

"These kids are crazy today. Plain crazy."

They had not gone.

"To kill a girl like that. Young and beautiful. Everything going for her."

The voices were coming closer.

"It's the booze, the drugs. The . . . Ah, let's go. It's been a long night."

"Yeah. A long one."

Suddenly he became rigid, and an icy wind swept over him. There was the startling beam of the searchlight, cutting through the darkness. It came near him. Now it was inches away. He huddled against the wall, waiting for the light to explode over him and for harsh words to spill out: *Put your hands up!*

Don't move!

Don't move or you're dead!

But the light went out and there was shivering silence. He waited, waited, and then for some strange reason time lost its logic and seemed to accelerate for him, and soon, soon, there was the sound of footsteps on the iron treads of the fire escape.

Then the slam of the car doors. One directly after the other.

The sound of the car moving again, and then he heard it no more.

9

He went down the fire escape and up the alley and then out onto the sidewalk. He looked warily about him, and then he started down the block, keeping close to the grey shadows and the darkness of the buildings and the unlit store fronts. He glanced at his wristwatch to see the time, and it gleamed in the darkness, and he thought of the moment he had been given the watch at the State Scholastic Swimming Championships. The glowing moment. The fine inscription on the back of the watch: Brian Cawley, one hundred meters. He grinned bitterly and walked along, a haunted look in his eyes.

It was close to four o'clock, and the streets of this lonely section were still empty and silent. He planned to go along the waterfront and then cut east into Soho. There was a chance he could make it to her place without being caught.

Dammit, he said fiercely to himself, I've got to make it.

But what if she won't help me?

What if she slams the door on me?

What if she calls the police?

He refused to answer the questions but went doggedly on, his arm hanging stiffly at his side, numb and aching. The bleeding had stopped a few hours ago, and he had taken the belt off. There was no longer any need for a tourniquet. The wound didn't look too bad. But at times he felt weak and dizzy, and his eyesight would blur just a bit, and he knew he'd have to get help. Somebody to help him before the night was up.

The bullet has to come out, Brian.

He passed a bar that was still open and the sound of the jukebox banging away with no one really listening to it made him feel inexpressibly sad and made him think of Donna and how she liked to listen to the music when it was low, always low. He thought he heard her voice, low and entreating, and he wanted to go into the bar and turn the music low, just low, for her.

For Donna.

Then he saw the police car, moving under the pillars of the West Side Highway, coming his way. He darted into a doorway and stood there taut in the darkness till it passed and was gone into the night. He came out again and ran a few blocks, close to the walls of the buildings, and then he turned up Christopher Street and after a short distance left it to go into the side streets that were more lonely and deserted.

He came to a derelict lying sprawled out in a doorway and next to him his old black felt hat and a torn bluish jacket. Brian stopped to stare at the grizzled, worn face, the mouth wide open, slack and open, showing a few straggly teeth, the gums, the closed eyes, and for a blinding instant he wanted to kick the man awake.

Kick him savagely and shout, Get up. Get up and take my place and I'll take yours. Give me your hat and jacket and I'll lie there in your spot. Let me just lie there. Your life is done for. Mine is just beginning. Get up and exchange lives with me. Damn you, you drunken lousy bum, get up and give me a chance at life. You've had yours and you blew it. Get up. Get up!

And then the madness left him. He bent down and picked up the old, grotesque hat and gently moved it closer to the sleeping man. He smiled wearily and went up the street, feeling the ache and stiffness in his arm. He passed a store front and he saw his reflection in the dark window and he stopped and gazed at it. He saw the ashen face and large eyes, and as he looked into the eyes, a memory came back to him of the eyes he had seen when he had gone hunting the last time with his father. The pleading eyes of a buck just after the bullet had smashed into his white furry chest, bringing him to his knees.

Pleading eyes. Pleading and lost.

They're my eyes now, he said to himself.

He turned away from the window and went on. And then he saw a phone booth on a deserted street corner and he went to it, saying to himself, I must not stop now. I must be going on. I can't be pushing my luck like this. I need every minute. I've got to get to her place. I've got to.

To Ellen Fisher.

To my old school teacher, Ellen Fisher.

She'll help me.

Like she did the last time. Five years ago.

I must not stop. Even for a second. I've got to get to her.

But he found himself putting the coins into the phone slot and dialing the number. And then listening to the ringing, and then the sudden snatching of the receiver off the hook and the low, anxious voice.

"Hello? Hello?"

"Mom," he said.

"Brian. Brian, where are you?"

"I'm all right, Mom."

"Brian."

And she couldn't speak.

"I'm all right," he said again.

"You're . . . hurt."

40

"No."

He could see her face, drained of color, white, so very white. Her trembling lips. The tears trickling down her cheeks.

And then he heard her voice again.

"Please."

"Mom, I'm not hurt. Not at all."

"They . . . they . . ."

"Mom, they missed me."

"Brian, the police were here. Brian. Brian."

He breathed out and didn't speak.

"Please."

And that was all she could say then.

"Mom, you know I didn't do it. You know it."

"Brian, where are you? Please."

"Mom, listen to me. I didn't. . . ."

And she cut in frantically. All her reserve was gone.

"Brian, where are you? You must give yourself up. Please do it before they kill you. Brian, I tell you, I plead with you. . . ."

Her voice choked up, and there was silence.

"Mom, for Christ sake, I didn't do it."

"You're wounded. You need help. Please."

"I'll be all right."

And then a sudden fear came over him and possessed him. He trembled. They were there, she said. What if they were tapping the phone? They could do that. They could put a tracer on this call.

They could be on their way here now.

I'd better get the hell out of the booth and start running again.

"Mom," he said. "I'm in Newark. I'll be all right."

Maybe they didn't have time to trace the call. Then she would tell them that. He was in Newark when he called me.

That's what he said. Newark.

"Brian, I beg you . . . I . . . beg. . . ."

She was sobbing. It tore through him.

"Good-bye, Mom. I love you."

41

"No. No."

"Good-bye."

"Brian, please don't leave me. Please. Please."

And he hung up, cutting off her voice. And as he did he remembered that not once did she say that she believed he was innocent.

Not once.

He stood there, as if suddenly someone had hit him hard in the chest. A hard, jarring blow, knocking the breath out of him. He slowly got out of the booth, face twisted with pain, and leaned against the folded glass door.

Who the hell cares if they get me or not, he thought.

Who cares?

What the hell's the use of it all?

Give in. Give up, you fool. You're a pigeon. You're lost. Forever lost.

And then he thought of Donna and how she was killed, and his jaw tightened, his eyes blazed, and he turned and hurried off into the night.

10

He was in Soho now and he passed the darkened art galleries, the closed boutiques and the silent loft buildings with their high arched windows. He passed a huge dim restaurant that was still open, he saw the small round tables, set with tablecloths, white as snow, and lit with tapering candles. No sound came from the restaurant. He saw a flicker of light, wavering light on a shadowed face, and then beyond it another small table and another shadowed face flecked with light, and then another till the last one merged into darkness. No one else was in the restaurant.

When he came to her block—a wide street with cobblestones that glistened—a dizziness and a nausea spread over him. He moved unsteadily into the gloom of an old loading platform and then sank down to the sidewalk in a sitting position, just under the platform's overhang.

I mustn't pass out now, he said to himself. If I do, I'm through. They'll find me here. I must keep my head down. The dizziness will pass if I keep my head down. I've got to get to her. I've got to.

He bent his head but kept his eyes open. He was

43

afraid if he closed them he would throw up and he didn't want that. That would have been the last indignity of all. He couldn't bear it.

A couple came out of one of the loft buildings and he heard the front door slam and then the high laughter of the woman and then he lifted his head and saw their figures cross the wide, cobbled street, swaying just a bit, their faces bright in the lamplight as they began to approach him, the man talking rapidly—a high-pitched voice, he had been drinking—and the woman laughing all the time. They walked by him without seeing him there in the darkness, and the man belched and the woman laughed again.

"You're drunk. Maybe you shouldn't drive."

"With my eyes closed."

And they both laughed. Then he saw them stop by a parked car and the man take out his keys and fumble with the lock till he finally opened the door and the two got into the car. And Brian remembered bitterly how the cops on the roof had slammed into the young for their drinking and drugs.

Those crazy kids.

He could still hear their voices floating down to him from the roof of the movie house. Their tired anger and contempt. And then he heard Donna's voice, soft and yet biting. They were sitting under the tree, their favorite tree, the summer sunshine filtering through the leafy branches.

"Everybody's blaming us," she said, her eyes flashing. "All the middle-aged saints. Staggering around with their cocktails and their pill bottles. Absurd. They're so absurd. My own father went to perform a brain operation and he was loaded, Brian. I tell you he was loaded."

"And how did it come out?"

"Fine. One of his best. Ah, people are so absurd, Brian. You know that. It's such a stupid, phony world we're living in. Going to kill us all one of these days."

"If we let it, Donna."

"Oh, hell, Brian. Why not let it? It's all a cosmic joke. Brian, Brian, you're smiling. It's a shame you're not in Philosophy One with me. Why are you a year younger than me and still in high school? Why? Why couldn't you have been a year older? And then we'd sit in Philosophy One, holding hands and saying life is a cosmic joke along with the bearded professor? Why, Brian?"

"Why, Donna?" he said out loud.

The car started up abruptly, the sound of the motor shattering the stillness. Then it sped to the corner, its red tail-lights glowing in the darkness, and then Brian saw the car round the corner, its tires squealing, and then the sound and the lights were snuffed out. All was still again. But he could still hear the laughing woman as he got to his feet and strangely it made him think of his mother and her white, drained face with the tears trickling down it.

"Absurd, Donna," he said sadly. "So damned absurd."

He leaned against the platform, his good hand gripping the wood. But the dizziness would not leave him. The dizziness and the searing anxiety. He pressed his lips together tight and started down the block, keeping close to the high walls and the blank doors of the buildings. He heard the sudden far off wail of an ambulance siren and he stopped and listened to it, eyes fixed, a cold tremor going through him, and he didn't start walking again until the sound completely vanished. Leaving no traces of itself.

Number 28.

This was where Ellen Fisher lived. He stood staring at the number on one of the green metal doors.

There was a naked electric bulb hanging over one of the doors and he stood before it, staring and swaying. 2 . . . 8.

Yes, he nodded slowly to himself, this is where she lives.

Number 28.

Then he looked slowly and warily about him to see if there was anybody else on the block, anybody who could see him go into the building, but there was nothing but darkness and spaced splashes of light.

The silent, neutral forms of parked cars.

A huge trailer truck, its windshield glimmering with lamplight.

He wanted to stand there and keep looking at the windshield—it was like a giant eye—but then he turned, an automatic movement, and put his hand to the knob of one of the doors. The coldness of the metal startled him. He shivered and then he turned the knob and the door opened and he entered the vestibule of the building.

The building was five stories high, and one of the floors was still being used as a pants factory. The other floors had been divided into loft apartments.

There was now another metal door facing him, but this one was locked. He turned to the house panel and looked for her name and button and as he did the thought came to him, vague and shimmering, that just a short time ago, maybe it was long ago, this very night, maybe it was some other night, he had gone into another vestibule and pressed another black button and his whole life changed.

Never to be the same again.

He pressed the button next to her name and leaned forward to hear. There was no answer. He pressed again, as hard as he could.

He waited and then he pressed the button a third time and now his panic and his weakness were overwhelming him.

What if she's not there?

What if she turns me away?

"Who is it?"

The voice was a woman's, harsh and angry.

"Donna," he said, and didn't realize what he was saying.

"Who?"

He trembled and then cried out in an agonized voice:

"Mrs. Fisher."

"Who is it? What do you want?"

"It—it's Brian. . . ."

And he couldn't go on. He wanted to break down and cry.

"Who are you?"

He leaned his hand against the panel and forced himself to speak.

"Brian Cawley—Brian Cawley . . . you—you once . . ."

She cut in sharply. "What? What did you say?"

"You—had me—in your class . . ."

"Brian Cawley?"

"Yes."

"Cawley?"

"Please, Mrs. Fisher. I . . . I'm hurt . . . I . . ."

"Brian?"

"I . . . I need . . . your help."

There was a silence, and again the dizziness and the nausea spread over him and he was sure that this time he would not be able to fight it down.

His eyes started to blur. His knees started to get weak.

"The second floor, Brian."

He heard the voice as from a great distance, and then the sound of the buzzer, harsh and abrupt and near, roused him.

It stopped and then started again.

He sighed out and then with a great effort straightened up again, using the wall for support.

"Second—floor," he muttered.

He went to the door and shoved it open. He let it swing shut and then leaned against it, gasping low.

His forehead was cold and wet.

"Ele . . . vator . . ."

He saw in a blur the open elevator to his right. It was a large freight elevator. Its outlines wavered. He moved slowly, unsteadily to it, stopped at the threshold and then went in.

His fingers groped for the button at 2.

"Mrs. Fisher . . . help . . . me . . ."

He stood swaying as the elevator went up slowly, ever slowly, to the second floor. Then it came to a grating halt.

He saw the door finally open, and he staggered out into the hallway. Then he saw her in a blur standing ahead of him.

"Brian."

She came quickly to him and put her strong arms about him. Then she helped him to her door and got him inside.

That was all he remembered.

11

When he opened his eyes, he was lying on a couch and a pale sun was filtering into the room. He felt a blanket over him, up to his chest, felt it with the fingers of his good arm. The other arm seemed light and weightless, detached, no longer a part of him. His fingers moved gently over the wool of the blanket, gently and sleepily, and were still. Then he saw a wooden chair, an old ladder-back wooden chair, near him, and on it a pair of scissors and a roll of bandage and then a bottle of peroxide and then a small bottle of pills and a glass of water, softly sparkling, and then a small tin oblong box of bicarbonate of soda and then he saw her figure and its large shadow on one of the walls.

She was standing near one of the high windows, just a bit beyond the chair. The sun glinted off her smooth black hair that was combed severely from her forehead and ended in a bun. The black hair had narrow streaks of grey in it.

"Just lie there. Don't move."

Her voice was quiet and authoritative. Her brown

eyes with the green flecks of light in them were scrutinizing him. Calmly and coldly.

"How do you feel?"

"Weak."

"Nauseous?"

"No."

"Chilled?"

"No."

"Any pain anymore in your arm?"

He hesitated and then answered.

"None."

"Still aches?"

"A bit."

"Any other pain or discomfort anywhere?"

"No."

"Just weak."

"Yes."

She smiled, a wintry smile, and then came slowly and thoughtfully over to him. She stood there looking down at him. He saw the Navaho pendant with the turquoise stones and then the wide silver bracelet on her wrist, and it sent a good feeling through him. He remembered how she always wore her American Indian jewelry in class on Mondays—every Monday, she started her week that way—and how she once told them of the summer she spent in a Navaho hogan near Window Rock. Spent it with the descendants of the Indians some of her ancestors had killed. The Arizona part of my family, she would say. The part that settled on the ranches.

We're the savages, she used to say, her brown eyes flashing fire. When it comes to the treatment of the Indians and all of our other minorities, we're the savages.

She put her hand to his forehead. It felt warm and comforting to him.

"You're coming along," she said.

"I'll be all right."

"Will you?"

Her eyes suddenly flashed and he thought she was

going to say more to him but she didn't. Her lips tightened. Then she moved away from him and stood in a shaft of sunlight, stocky and secure, just as she used to stand at the head of the class, looking quietly and severely at the faces of everybody in the room.

He heard her voice come to him.

"I've cleaned the wound, Brian. There should be no infection."

He wanted to ask her when she had done it. He had no memory of it. And then he did, of her face blurred in the lamplight, his crying out in pain as a penetrating icy liquid was poured over the wound, her tender arm about him, raising him to drink something acrid tasting, and then his falling back into a well of darkness and sweet sleep.

"No infection," she said again, her voice low and level.

He lay there watching her. Her face had small regular features, delicate features, yet there was always a sense of quiet strength to it. Her eyes attracted and fascinated him. The changing lights in them. He used to sit in the classroom and stare at them. She must've been a very beautiful woman when she was young, he thought.

Ellen Fisher.

Ellen.

He never thought of her as Mrs. Fisher. Always Ellen. He had been in love with her when he was twelve. The first time he came into class and saw her. And then he had moved back from the city to Elton, and there Donna began slowly and imperceptibly to move to the center of his life. Ellen Fisher became Mrs. Fisher in his memory.

He heard her voice again.

"Brian."

"Yes, Mrs. Fisher."

"I come from a farm."

"I know," he murmured.

She had often spoken of the farm to the class. That

51

small dairy farm, isolated and alone, in the back areas of northern Minnesota.

"Grew up on one and have been going back to one for the past thirty-five years. I know bullets and guns. Have used a shotgun myself more than once."

He waited.

"I know a bullet wound when I see it."

He tried to look away from her searching eyes but he couldn't. They held him.

"My husband was killed by one. Went out hunting and a damn fool shot him for a deer." Her eyes crackled. "I know a bullet wound when I see one."

"It's a bullet," he said.

"It is, Brian."

He lay back and didn't say anything. He wanted to close his eyes and sleep. Just sleep and forget everything.

"Everything," he murmured in a very low and weary voice.

"Who shot you?"

He closed his eyes.

"Brian."

He opened his eyes, and he looked past her and saw the kitchen alcove of the apartment and the glitter and play of sunlight on a neat row of aluminum pots hanging on the brick wall, and he thought with a sinking heart of his mother standing in the kitchen of their home, tall and dark-haired and hollow-eyed, making coffee.

She always drank lots of coffee when she was worried and fearful. Cup after cup.

"Who, Brian?"

What was she doing now? Who was with her now?

"Brian."

Mrs. Fisher's voice cut through to him.

"The police," he whispered.

Her face became tight and cold, and she was silent. From outside came the rumble of a heavy truck on the cobblestone street. He listened to it, frantically, till the sound thinned away and was lost.

"Why?"

She had come closer to him. He began to fear her.

"I didn't do anything wrong, Mrs. Fisher. I didn't."

"Why, Brian?"

"I tell you I. . . ."

"Why, Brian?"

Her voice was now cruel and imprisoning.

"Donna is dead."

"Donna?"

And then he realized that she had never met Donna. Never knew her. Never loved her. And now he felt completely lost and destroyed.

"Donna?" she asked again.

"Please, Mrs. Fisher. . . ."

He choked up and couldn't speak. And he said to himself bitterly, I was a damn fool to come here. She won't help me. She'll turn me over to the police and it will be over.

I'm a pigeon.

He closed his eyes. And lay there in agonized silence. He fought desperately to keep the tears back.

But he felt them cold and wet on his eyelids.

"Brian," she said gently, and her voice was now close to him.

He slowly opened his eyes.

"Brian Cawley."

She sat down on the couch near him and then took two pills from the small bottle. Then she picked up the glass of water.

"Take this," she said.

He raised his head a bit and let her put the pills into his mouth. Then she put her arm about him—he felt its instant warmth and security—and she lifted him up a bit more.

"Drink the water."

He swallowed the pills and then drank the water slowly, and all the time he wanted to stay there that way, just to feel her warm, comforting arm about him.

"Good."

She slowly eased him back onto the couch again

53

and then stood up and gazed long at him. She sighed gently.

"The bullet has to come out, Brian."

He felt a ripple of fear pass over him.

"You have to see a doctor for that. The police have to be notified. It's the law. You know that."

"They killed Donna," he said.

"Who killed her, Brian?"

He didn't answer.

"It's not right," he murmured. "It's not right."

He turned his head away from her.

"Brian," she said. "I have to call the police. I could be in trouble already for not calling them before. You understand that, don't you?"

"Donna is dead," he said, and his voice almost broke. "And the police want to. . . ."

He couldn't finish.

"Brian, it's no use. The police have to be notified."

He turned to her.

"And I'll be thrown into jail. For years and years."

"Why will you be thrown into jail? What did you do?"

"Nothing. But they think I killed Donna."

Her face paled. Her hands clenched and then slowly opened again.

"You?"

"How could I? I loved Donna. With all my heart."

"You a murderer? Brian Cawley?" She shook her head fiercely. "No. Not you."

He looked up at her, and a great plea came into his eyes. He reached out his hand to her, touched her and then let it fall to his side.

"Please listen to me. Please. You helped me when I came to you. Almost five years ago. Do you remember?"

She didn't answer.

"Do you?"

"Yes, Brian."

He raised his hand to her, and when he spoke, his

words came out in a flow. For deep within he knew he was fighting for his life.

And for Donna.

"My folks were breaking up and I didn't know where to turn. Who to love. Who to blame. What was really going on. My mother moved here from Elton and I was all alone with her and my father had taken off for good. Forever. He was my idol all my life. Without a damn word to me. Not a solitary word. Like I had committed a crime. Like it was my fault that they didn't love each other anymore. My fault."

She was silent and he went on.

"I didn't know what to do. It was ripping me apart. Day and night. Never a letup. I was ready to kill myself. To slit my wrists. To jump in front of a subway train. I almost did. And . . . and you saw my agony and made me come here to talk to you. You would comfort me. Again and again. And you made me feel loved and wanted and understood and you pulled me through. No psychiatrist could've done what you did. You saved my life. My head. I know it now. You did, Mrs. Fisher. You did."

He stopped speaking and fell back onto the couch again. His face lean and pale and damp. The room was still.

"And that's why you came to me now, Brian," she said softly, almost to herself.

"There was no one to turn to. There was no one to go to. No one. I called my mother and she thinks I'm guilty. I. . . ."

"I'm sure she doesn't, Brian."

But he didn't seem to hear her.

"No one to turn to," he said. "No one. Then I thought of you. Even while I was running from the police I thought of you. I said to myself she would help me. I just knew you'd be here, to help me. I knew it."

"But, Brian . . ."

"You can."

She shook her head sadly.

"I can't."

He raised himself on one elbow. His face was taut with pain and emotion.

"Please help me. I'm begging you."

"It's impossible, Brian."

"Why impossible? You can. You can." And a wild look came into his eyes and he suddenly cried out, "Why didn't you call the police before?"

She stared at him.

"Why, Mrs. Fisher?"

"Why?"

"Yes. Yes."

"My first thought was to take care of you."

"But you knew it was a bullet wound."

She slowly nodded.

"And yet you didn't call the police. A bullet wound, Mrs. Fisher."

She stood there looking at him, and then she finally spoke.

"I guess I wanted to hear your side, Brian," she said.

"Will you?"

"I'll still have to call the police."

"No," he shouted. "No."

She came over to him quickly.

"Brian, lie down. This is not good for you."

But he wouldn't move.

"You won't call them," he cried out. "Not after you hear my side. Not after that. I know you won't. I know it."

She put her two arms firmly about him.

"Lie still and rest," she said grimly. "Not another word."

He lay back on the couch again. She released him and stood up. Then she turned and walked away from him and stood by the window, staring down at the street. He could see her sturdy figure and the sunlight glinting on her hair.

After a while, he called to her in a low voice.

"Mrs. Fisher."

"Yes, Brian?"

She didn't turn from the window.

"I feel awfully tired and sleepy."

"I guess you would."

"Will you promise me something?"

"What is it, Brian?"

"That you won't send for the police while I sleep?"

She slowly turned from the window.

"I'll do nothing until I hear your side, Brian," she said.

"Thank you, Mrs. Fisher," he murmured.

Then he closed his eyes.

12

"And then the voice said, Run, pigeon, run."

"And you ran."

"What else could I do?"

She was silent.

"What chance did I have? Everything was stacked against me."

"But your running away was an admission of guilt, Brian."

"And staying there meant being brought into court and tried and sentenced. The jury would've convicted me in ten minutes. Don't you see I had no choice but to run? I was guilty if I stayed or if I ran."

She sat across from him in an old wide armchair, her strong hands quiet in her lap. The late afternoon shadows, slanting and long, were on the wooden floor and brick walls of the loft. He looked past her to where the huge room stretched to a sunny area where he could see two wooden pedestals and on them two pieces of sculpture in different stages of progress. One was the head and upper torso of a man, the face rugged and sad. It was of clay. The other, of grey veined stone, had not yet taken a definite form. Beyond the pedestals were two high windows that looked out onto an empty stretch of sky, and then beyond that he saw the walls and sun-burnished windows of another loft building.

She had propped him up on the couch with a pillow behind him. The dressing had been changed, and she had fed him hot soup and some tea and toast.

He felt stronger and more hopeful. But the wound in the arm still ached.

"I ran and I got shot and I came here."

"No one saw you come into this building?"

"The block was empty. I made sure to look around."

"And the voice on the phone?"

"I never heard it before. And I don't know why he warned me."

"Nor why Donna was killed?"

"No."

"Or why you were set up as a pigeon?"

"Some strange ideas have been coming to me. I've been lying here trying to remember things about Donna and me . . . and some of her friends."

"What about her friends?"

He hesitated and then spoke.

"I don't know. I couldn't really get a fix on them. There was something weird and. . . ."

His voice trailed off into silence.

"How do you mean weird? Drugs?"

"Not that so much. Their—their politics. Kind of way out. Like they were into some real wild things."

"Like murder?"

He didn't answer.

"And Donna was mixed up with them?"

"In a way."

"How do you mean, Brian?"

"I—I've got to think more—I really don't know."

"Oh."

They were silent.

"Do you believe what I've told you, Mrs. Fisher?" he suddenly asked.

She nodded.

"Yes, Brian."

"That I'm innocent?"

"I do."

He leaned forward to her.

"Then if you believe that how can you turn me over to the police?"

"Do you know, Brian, if I keep you any longer I can go to jail?"

He didn't answer.

"I'm in trouble already for what I've done. Just look at me, Brian, and look at what you're asking."

"But I'm innocent."

"I believe that, Brian."

She sat there gazing at him, a soft, searching look in her hazel eyes. When she spoke again, her voice was low and appealing.

"Brian, listen to me. Please. I'm a retired schoolteacher who lives in Soho and is enjoying her well-deserved rest after a long lifetime of hard teaching. And it can be hard, Brian. It can." Her voice faded out into silence. And then she began again. "I've always wanted to do sculpture. Not on Sundays and vacation time. But all the time. It was a hunger with me. A desperate hunger. Do you understand that?"

"Yes," he murmured.

"I'm finally doing what I want. I'm a widow. I have no children." She pointed to the two pedestals. "I have that. A few good friends. Good health and some years ahead of me."

He couldn't look at her when he spoke.

"All I'm asking is a chance," he said.

"And I would very much like to give you that chance."

"But you can't. And you won't. I want to find out who killed Donna. That will save my life and let her have peace. I know she's not resting. I . . ." His voice broke and then he said, "I have to find them. I just have to find them."

60

She sat there, and a profound look of sadness and despair settled over her face and her strong figure.

"Yes," she whispered. "I guess you have to."

Outside the street was quiet. Finally she sighed.

"And how would you go about finding Donna's killers?"

He looked up at her.

"I'm sure they're in the Village or in Soho," he said. "They're here."

"Why are you sure?"

"I went to a Village party with Donna. I got into an argument with one of her friends. And that's how Donna and I broke up."

"Until last night when she phoned you."

"Yes."

"She wanted to see you. It was something urgent. Did she tell you what it was about?"

"No. Only that she wanted to see me. And I saw her."

He held his breath as he said the last words and bowed his head in pain. She knew that he was back in the bleak light of Donna's apartment, standing there and looking down at her.

She waited and then spoke again.

"Tell me more about Donna's friends."

He raised his head to her. His grey eyes were distant.

"Her friends?"

"Yes. Their politics. Their way of looking at life. Try and think, Brian."

"Oh," he said.

"Think, Brian."

"I know them mostly through what Donna said about them. And what I saw and heard at that party. They're people who've given up on life. Do you know what I mean?"

"I think so."

His lips thinned in anger.

"They talk of a better world, and I agree with them there. This world is a pretty stinking place when you

61

take a good hard look at it. But they don't really want to do anything to change things. With them it's all talk and hate. When you really get down to it, they want no world. No world at all."

He paused and then went on. "It's all a bunch of crap to them. They believe in nothing. Not even in themselves. The human being is a clown. To be born is—is an absurdity. That's how they put it. Absurd."

"And Donna?"

He shook his head fiercely.

"Donna was never comfortable with them. She went along for the ride. It was just another experience for her. Deep down, Donna loved life and had faith in human beings. She would never really face that truth and admit it."

And in the end she paid for it, Mrs. Fisher thought sadly.

"They're college students, Brian?"

"Most of them. Some have graduated and sit around doing nothing."

"Go on."

"I think Donna wanted to get out."

"To get out of what, Brian?"

He hesitated and then spoke wearily.

"I don't know. But it was something terrible. Something that frightened her."

"Brian," she said. "If you feel they are the ones who killed Donna, then they can kill you."

He looked at her and then smiled a slow, despairing smile.

"Haven't they already?" he said.

She sighed gently.

"I know what you mean."

He leaned forward to her.

"Just give me the chance to go after them. To find out something about them. Maybe then I can turn myself in. I'll have a chance. Help me."

"I'd like to, Brian," she said.

"I've got nothing to lose. Nothing. What more can they do to me? What more can they take from me?"

"You could be wrong. Your theory about Donna's friends all wrong. Someone else could well be her murderer."

"I know they are the killers."

"You don't know it, Brian."

He shook his head doggedly.

"Then give me the chance to find out."

"I'm not to call the police. Is that it, Brian?"

"Yes. That's it, Mrs. Fisher."

"And the bullet that's in your arm?"

"The bullet?"

"Well, Brian?"

But she didn't wait for him to answer. She rose and went over to a small table and picked up a folded newspaper. Then she came back to him with it.

"Today's edition," she said quietly.

He didn't take the newspaper from her hand. Just sat there waiting for her to speak.

"Brian, while you slept I stepped out to do some shopping. To get some medicines and bandages. Also to sound out some of my neighbors and to find out if you were seen in the area last night. You haven't been seen, Brian."

She held up the newspaper and then opened it.

"But you have made page three of the *New York Post*. Picture and all."

He looked silently at his picture and saw the words: Killer Sought. He trembled and turned away from her for a moment.

"Your mother has told the police that you phoned her from Newark. They're searching for you there."

"I thought she would," he said bitterly.

"She begs you to go to the police."

"No," he said.

"For your own good. She knows you have been shot and that the police are waiting for you to show up at some hospital emergency room. Or some doctor's office."

"No," he said again.

"She's on your side, Brian."

"Is she?"

"Read what she has to say. How much she loves you."

Mrs. Fisher dropped the newspaper onto the couch, close to him, and went back to her chair. She was about to sit down again when he spoke.

"You can take out the bullet for me."

She turned sharply to him.

"I?"

"You can do it. I know you can. If you want to."

"I don't want to, Brian."

She slowly sat down on the chair again.

"Mrs. Fisher," he said. "You're forgetting something."

"What is it, Brian?"

"Something I never forgot. I guess you were too good a teacher."

"What is it, Brian?" she asked again, her voice sharp and low.

"About the time your father saved an Indian's life one winter. During a bad snowstorm. It was in the woods not too far from your farm. You were a small girl then, you said."

"You remembered that?"

"There are Indians in Minnesota, aren't there?"

"There are."

"We in the class never knew that. And you also told the class that was how you first became interested in the American Indian and his history and his savage destiny. Those are your words. I never forgot them."

"I don't remember, Brian," she said, her face pale.

But he knew that she did.

"You said your father told you, Once you have saved a life you are responsible for it for all time to come. Because a great act of goodness binds one to a life with cords that cannot be cut or broken. Your father said that was an old Indian legend."

Her face was set hard like a mask. But the eyes were sad and haunting.

"The Indian came back, didn't he?"

"Yes," she said.

"And your father helped him again, didn't he?"

"Yes," she said.

"I've come back, Mrs. Fisher."

"I don't want to take the hullet out, Brian," she said.

"Mrs. Fisher."

"No."

"It's not too deep."

She shook her head grimly.

"I can stand the pain," he said.

"No."

"I can, I tell you."

"I will not do it, Brian."

"You saved my life once, Mrs. Fisher. I'm asking you to do it again."

They sat staring at each other in an absolute stillness. The late shadows hovered about them.

On the pedestal the dying sun caught the face of the rugged man and lit it. Somehow Brian knew it was the face of her father.

13

She gave him another shot of Old Granddad bourbon. She watched him as he drank it down. This time he didn't grimace. The bourbon was going down smoothly. I believe I've given him enough, she thought. He lay back on the couch and closed his eyes.

"How do you feel?" she asked.

"Good," he said.

"Numb?"

"Sort of. And sort of silly. I want to laugh."

"You're not going to do much laughing," she said.

"I know. But that's how I feel."

"Stretch out your arm on the chair. You can keep your eyes closed or open. Just as you wish."

"I'll open them for a while."

"The arm, Brian."

She had spread a clean white towel over the seat of the wooden chair. And on another chair next to it she had placed a gleaming pot of boiling water and in it the instruments she was going to use. He had watched her take a darning needle and with a pair of steel pliers bend the pointed tip into a hook form. And then he had watched her take a pair of tweezers and work on it until she had the ends shaped as she wanted them. And while he watched her with the other preparations, he thought of the wide, sunlit kitchen of the farmhouse. And he saw her sewing up the gashed leg of one of the farmhands who had been hired for the early fall's cutting. She had told the class of the incident.

And of others.

Life on a Minnesota farm can be pretty primitive, she had said. Harsh and demanding. You are sometimes forced to do things you never thought you were capable of doing. Especially if you're way up where we were settled. You could just as well be back in the early years of the last century, particularly after the heavy snows came.

"What music would you like to hear?"

"Now?"

"Yes. It will distract you and calm me."

"You don't need any music to calm you, Mrs. Fisher," he said.

She smiled bleakly.

"I may not look it. Or show it. But I need it."

She went to the front windows and closed them. She came back and sat on the arm of the couch.

"Well, Brian?"

He shrugged slightly.

"It doesn't matter. Pick what you want."

"All right. The Sibelius First Symphony."

"Okay with me."

"Do you know it?"

"Just a bit."

"Well, here's a chance to get real close to it. I'm going to put it on quite loud."

"Loud?"

"Very loud, Brian."

She got up, and his eyes followed her as she went to the record player that was on the lower shelf of a wall bookcase. He watched her take a record from an

67

album and then set it onto the turntable. Soon he heard the opening strains of the symphony.

The opening, hauntingly beautiful strains.

And he began to remember the symphony and the last time he had heard it. He had gone to a concert with Donna at NYU's Loeb Center. It was during the past winter and it was snowing and Eric Leinsdorf was the conductor of the orchestra, and Donna and he had come late and missed a Beethoven overture, and the snow, the snow, was still glistening and melting on Donna's hair . . .

Her shimmering wet hair.

Her hair.

And he said to himself wearily, painfully, Why is it that everything I do or that is done to me reminds me of Donna?

Everything.

He put his good hand into one of the pockets of his Levi's, and he drew out the locket. The golden locket he had once given Donna. The locket he had taken from her last night as she lay silent, forever silent, on the couch. He held it up in the glowing sunlight, and then he closed his hand about the flashing gold, closed it tight.

Mrs. Fisher turned the volume higher, and the music began to well up about them. The icy realization now came to him with full force, the realization that she was making the music this loud so the neighbors would not hear him when he began to scream in pain.

She went into the bathroom, leaving the door open, and he saw her go over to the sink and begin to wash her hands thoroughly like a surgeon before an operation, and then he saw her carefully dry her hands. He watched her come out of the bathroom and approach him.

And he felt fear, fear of pain.

She spoke to him and he heard her, clearly and distinctly, against the background of the music.

"I guess we're about ready, Brian."

"Yes," he said.

"You can still back out."

"No."

She seemed to see his fear.

"You wouldn't feel as much pain in a hospital. They have the equipment and the means to deaden pain. To make it bearable."

"No," he said.

"All I have is bourbon. And I won't give you any more."

"Why are you doing this to me?" he said harshly. "It's not fair, Mrs. Fisher."

She looked at him, and her face became red.

"Yes. You're right," she said. "Forgive me."

"Let's get on with it."

She put her hand tenderly on his hair and softly stroked it.

"You're right."

"Do you think I should have another whiskey?" he asked.

She shook her head gently, still stroking his hair.

"No. You have about enough in you already. Too much is no good."

"Whatever you say," he murmured.

"I'll have to wash my hands again after touching your hair," she said.

"Mrs. Fisher."

She turned to him.

He opened his hand with the locket shining in its palm.

"Could you do me a favor?"

"What is it, Brian?"

He hesitated and then spoke.

"I'd like to wear this locket. While you . . . you. . . ."

She came over to him.

"I understand.".

"Could you put it on for me? Please?"

"Yes, Brian," she said, and he thought her voice shook.

He bent his head, and she opened the chain and then set it about his neck and closed the clasp.

"Thanks," he said.

She stroked his hair again and then turned and went to the bathroom sink. This time he saw her wash her face along with her hands. Then she came out of the room and over to him.

Her face was now stern and concentrated.

"Are you ready, Brian?"

"Yes."

She began to probe into the wound. And it was when the music began its last surge, close to the end of the first movement, very close to it, he remembered it was then, yes, it was then that he found himself screaming.

14

He woke a few times during the night calling for her, and she came to him. But just as the long darkness was giving way to morning light, he fell into a deep, restful sleep. And when he woke from that sleep, he felt light and almost gay.

He looked for her, and he saw her sitting in her chair, her head down and her eyes closed. But he could see her face, and it was tired and drawn. Her hands hung loose over her lap. The strong hands were now weak and vulnerable.

She looks so desperately tired, he thought with sadness and guilt. And I am doing this to her. He was about to close his eyes again when he heard her voice.

"Good evening, Brian."

She seemed to sense that he had been awake.

"Evening?"

"Yes. It is almost that."

"I can't believe it."

"You've been sleeping a long, long time. How do you feel?"

"Fine."

"Dizzy? Nauseous? A little?"

He shook his head and smiled.

"No. Just fine."

"And you're in a good mood."

"Uh-huh."

"Any pain in your arm?"

He lay there and thought.

"Just aches a bit, I guess."

"A bit."

"Uh-huh."

"That's to be expected. Let me take a look at it."

She got up very slowly, stretched her arms, stifled a yawn, and then came over to him. Her eyes, though still tired-looking, were now bright and calm, and he wondered at her great strength. He waited patiently while she cut the bandages from the arm. Her fingers searched delicately about the edges of the wound, and once he winced.

"Am I hurting you?"

"No."

"Just a bit?"

"It's all right."

She pressed tenderly at the flesh, watching his face all the time.

"Don't play the hero, Brian. I must have the truth."

"I'm not."

Her eyes twinkled, and he felt her warmth spread through him. It made him feel less lonely and lost.

"The young are always dramatizing themselves, aren't they?" she said.

"Why not?"

She laughed softly and echoed him.

"Why not?"

She took her fingers away and nodded.

"It looks fine to me. No infection."

"Did you expect one, Doctor?"

She began putting a new dressing over the wound.

"No. But there's always a possibility."

"Even with the best of doctors."

"Even with the best."

"And you're the best," he said gently, fervently.

72

Her face flushed, and she was silent. Down on the street sidewalk some children were playing in the evening sunlight. Their high, thin voices drifted up to them.

She spoke to him.

"You'll be on your feet in another day. And then what?"

"And then it's my turn," he said grimly.

She looked up at him, her eyes measuring his taut face, and then she continued bandaging the arm.

"Brian," she said.

"Yes, Mrs. Fisher?"

"I want you to do me a favor."

"Sure. What is it?"

But he wondered what it was she now wanted of him. Wondered and almost feared.

"I'm going to give you a pen and some paper, and you're going to write a letter."

"A letter? To whom?"

"Your mother."

"No," he said.

"You'll tell her that you're well. Somebody competent helped you. Believes in you. And will help you prove your innocence."

He stared at her and didn't speak.

"And that you love her," she said quietly.

"But, Mrs. Fisher, you don't understand. I . . ."

She shook her head firmly, cutting him off.

"I want you to do that, Brian."

"She doesn't believe in me."

"Brian."

"She doesn't. I tell you she doesn't."

Ellen Fisher silently finished bandaging the arm. Then without a word to him she rose, and he watched her go to an old oak desk that stood against one of the brick walls and open the top drawer and take out two sheets of blank white paper. She went to her black leather purse, opened it, and took out a silver pen. She shut the purse, and he heard the sharp click. Then he saw her come over to him.

73

"I'm going to put this on the chair here, Brian," she said, and he remembered her speaking in that tone of voice and in the very same manner years ago in her classroom.

"I can't do it," he said.

She put the pen and the two sheets of paper on the wooden chair next to him. The pen was an old one, the silver had dulled, and he somehow felt that her father had given it to her when she was a young girl graduating from school. He could see her initials engraved in scroll letters. The initials were E. H. Her name had been Ellen Harper before she was married.

"You will, Brian," she said.

"My mother's helping the police. Helping them to catch me and put me away for the rest of my life. Can't you see that?" he said bitterly.

"Your mother loves you. And her heart is breaking, Brian."

"That's not so."

"It is so."

He shook his head and clenched his hand and didn't speak to her.

"She believes in you," Mrs. Fisher said gently.

"No," he said. "No. She believes I can kill a person. A person I cared for. A . . . she . . ." His voice broke and he couldn't go on.

"I want you to write that letter."

"No," he murmured.

"I'll go to Newark. It's a short ride across the river by the tubes. I'll mail the letter from a mailbox there."

"She'll turn the letter over to the police."

"No harm will be done. They'll still think you're hiding out in Newark, and that's what you want. It will make it easier for you to move around here in the Village."

He looked away from her to the kitchen wall and the aluminum pots hanging there in a neat shining row, and he saw his mother again. She was sitting in their kitchen, a cup of coffee on the small table, her dark head bowed, waiting for the phone to ring.

He felt a twinge of pain in his heart and yearning for her.

"Mom," he whispered.

But then he fought it all down and turned away from the wall.

Outside the children had gotten into a quarrel, and their voices sounded like the sharp cries of angry birds.

"He's safe." "No, he's not." "The ball hit him." "It didn't."

"The ball hit him," Brian said tonelessly, and he wished he could be down there playing with them. Just as small and alive and free of fears as they were. Wished that the years could be wiped out and that he could be down there in the evening sun. . . .

He heard her voice.

"Well, Brian?"

"Let me think a while," he said.

"All you want. But you'll write that letter."

"I don't know yet."

"It's an assignment, and you'll do it," she said sharply.

"I'm not back in school," he said fiercely.

She stood there in front of him, sturdy and immovable.

"You're back in my school, Brian," she said. "The minute you walked through that door and involved me in your life you were back in my school. And you'll do from now on what I say." Her voice lashed out at him. "What I say, Brian Cawley."

He stared up at her and almost trembled.

"Is that clear to you?"

He slowly nodded.

"Yes, Mrs. Fisher."

"That's more like it," she said grimly. "After you write that letter, we'll sit down and talk."

"All right."

"You'll tell me all you remember about Donna's friends, where you believe they usually hang out."

He nodded silently.

"I've been working over a plan on how you can walk

75

the streets and not be recognized by them or the police."

"You have, Mrs. Fisher?"

But she didn't answer him.

"How many of her friends know you?"

"None of them really know me."

"You're sure of that?"

"Yes."

"How about the one you had words with?"

"It was over in a flash. I could walk up to him and he wouldn't recognize me. I was just another guy at a crowded, smoky party. The only one I ever went to. I guess he felt I had a drink too many. None of them know me. I'm safe that way."

"But you would know them?"

"Yes," he said, and his face became tight. "They're in my mind all the time."

"Good. Your picture was in the newspaper, Brian. You're forgetting that. You could be recognized from your picture."

"I could," he said. "But I'll have to take that chance."

"You don't have to."

"What do you mean?"

She didn't answer him but went over to her chair and sat down. Her face was sombre and thoughtful.

"How about the murderer?" he suddenly asked. "He knocked me out and then soaked me with whiskey. He might recognize me."

"I've thought about that, too," she said. "I've been thinking of all the possibilities, Brian. Been thinking for many hours." She paused and then went on, this time in a gentle but firm voice. "Now remember, Brian. You are out to get information that hopefully will clear you. Just that and nothing else. And you are to be very, very careful in everything that you do. You are not to lose your temper and take any stupid chances."

"I won't lose my temper," he said almost sullenly.

"Make sure of that. And forget revenge."

"Revenge?" he said in a bitter voice.

"Your first consideration is to keep yourself alive. And after that to establish your innocence." Her voice became sharp. "Remember that, Brian."

"Yes, Mrs. Fisher," he said.

And he was about to speak again, but she motioned him to be silent. Then she seemed to come to a decision.

"There are some clothing stores in the Village where one can pick up special outfits to wear. I'll take a walk to one of them."

"And?"

She sat there studying him, and then she nodded her head curtly.

"I'll have to dye your hair blond."

"Blond? Why?"

"Yes. That should do it. What's your waist size?"

"Thirty-two or thirty-three."

"And your jacket size?"

"Forty should do it."

"Yes. You do have wide shoulders," she said approvingly. "Is that from your swimming, Brian?"

"I guess so."

"Have you ever ridden a motorcycle?"

"What?"

"Have you?"

"I still own a small Honda," he said.

She smiled.

"Good. Then you'll know how to talk about it should the need arise."

"I haven't used it in a while," he said.

"Why not?"

He shrugged.

"Got sort of tired of the whole thing. Still don't know why I bought it." And then he said, "Donna thought it would be a thrill. Yes. It was that. It was Donna."

She gazed at the locket he wore and a wistful look came over her face for an instant, and then she spoke again.

77

"You probably know a lot about the motorcycle gangs?"

"You mean like Hell's Angels and the Outlaws? And the other crazy groups knocking around?"

She smiled, but her hazel eyes were cold.

"Yes. I've often seen these characters walking the Village streets and sitting in the dark coffeehouses and the little bars. All dressed up in their breeches, black boots, leather vests, visored caps and smoked glasses."

She paused and then said to him, "I believe that's the outfit you'll be waring."

He gaped at her. "Me?"

"But you'll be from a group out on the Coast. I saw a number of them out in San Francisco two years ago. The Aryans."

"Aryans?"

"You've never heard of them?"

He shook his head. "No."

"They dye their hair blond and wear the Iron Cross. I've never seen any of them East yet. They're local and keep to their territory. They have a shack in Sausalito. That's their only headquarters. So you'll be pretty safe wearing their getup. You won't come across any of them in the Village or Soho."

"The Iron Cross was never one of my favorite decorations," he said.

"Nor mine, Brian. But it might be to some of the characters you're looking for."

"I see what you mean," he murmured.

"The Aryans as far as I can judge are not Nazis. They play at it. The trouble with the world today is that too many people, especially some of the young, are playing at things. And then sooner or later they stop playing and start doing things. Like Donna's friends. And I am now beginning to believe that Donna played for a while and then wanted out when the playing stopped. And they wouldn't let her out. It was too late then."

"They wouldn't let her out," he said, his face pale and grey.

"I believe that's what happened, Brian. She belonged to some group. A group that stopped playing games."

They were silent.

"But I'm not playing," he suddenly blurted out. "It's not a game to me. It's my life."

"I know, Brian."

"And Donna's."

She sat there, her hands quiet in her lap, her figure solid and controlled; then she rose and came over to him.

"Well, Brian. We are now in this together. All the way."

He looked up at her.

"You're putting yourself on the line for me. You could lose everything, Mrs. Fisher. And yet you're doing this."

She said nothing, just touched his hair gently and turned and went to her purse.

"I'll go out and buy some of the things you'll be needing. You try to rest."

"Okay," he said.

She paused in the doorway and turned to him.

"Brian."

"Yes?"

Outside the children had finished their game and had left the sidewalk and gone to their homes. A car passed, and then the evening street was quiet again.

"Do you remember when I once read the life of Julius Caesar to the class?"

Her eyes glowed and the lights in them changed, and he thought how beautiful she must have been when she was a young girl.

"I've crossed my Rubicon, Brian," she said softly.

Then she went out closing the door behind her.

15

The rain swept down over the dark side street. Brian pulled the wet, glistening visor of his cap over his eyes and then slowly crossed to the blinking lights of the coffeehouse. He read the words of the electric sign, The Blue Candles. Yes, that was one of their hangouts, he said to himself. He had never been there, but he had heard Donna once mention the name, The Blue Candles, and then he had forgotten it. But now he found himself remembering everything. Again and again. His mind feverishly went over and over every little moment he had ever spent with Donna. Every word she had ever spoken to him.

Every gesture she had ever made.

He paused in the empty doorway, took off his dark glasses and carefully wiped them dry with his handkerchief and then put them on again. He went inside and sat down at one of the small round tables. There were tall blue candles in shallow glass holders on each of the tables. The tiny golden flames of the candles wavered and cast flickering shadows on the walls. The walls were grey and bare. And at one end of the low-ceilinged room was a small stage, narrow and bare, and on it a lean fellow sat on an old folding chair, playing a guitar and singing a soft slow song. He didn't use a microphone. The words of the song, a mountain ballad, drifted in broken snatches to Brian.

A young slight girl in jeans and a faded blue T-shirt came over to Brian's table. She stood there waiting for his order. She had a round pert face, and her eyes were bright and dark. She was no more than eighteen or nineteen, Brian surmised.

"What's it going to be?"

He just sat there, casually appraising her. She asked again, and he took his time before answering.

"A cappuccino," he finally said.

"That's it?"

"You heard it once," he drawled and grinned.

She smiled at him. She seemed to like his curt, easy, offhand manner.

"And it's still cappuccino."

"Still."

"And that's what you're going to get."

"That's what I expect."

"Where are you from?"

"West."

"How far west?"

"As far as you can go."

"Los Angeles?"

"Frisco."

"Never been there. Never been past Chicago."

"I've got a bike. Want to go? It's a smoking Honda."

"I'll think it over."

Her eyes were dancing. She was enjoying him.

"What do you do in the daytime?" he asked.

"I go to NYU. Social studies."

"Like it?"

She nodded.

"It's a great school. This is a hangout for a lot of students."

"I see."

She stood there smiling at him, still not wanting to

leave him and get his order. He pushed his cap back and gazed up at her. She looks so innocent, he thought. And yet she could be part of them.

On the stage the guitar player finished the song and then reached down and picked up a bottle of beer that was at his side and drank thirstily from it.

He set the bottle down again and then began a new ballad. Nobody in the room seemed to pay any attention to him.

"How's business tonight?" Brian asked.

"Not so good. The rain's too heavy."

"It'll let up soon," he said.

"Hope so. I like your hair."

"I like it, too," he said.

"What kind of eyes do you have? Can't tell behind those glasses."

"Blue in the daytime and grey at night."

She laughed.

"You're fresh and cute, aren't you?"

"I'm cute."

"And the girls spoil you, don't they?"

"Some of them."

"And this cross that you're wearing?"

"I won it in battle."

He thought her eyes had glinted for an instant when she asked him about the Iron Cross. But he wasn't sure.

"You're cute. It's hard to tell your age. You could be eighteen or twenty-six. Which is it?" she asked.

"Both," he said.

"You're cute," she said and left him.

Brian got up and took off his leather jacket and hung it over one of the chairs. He kept his cap on and his dark glasses. He wore a long-sleeved yellow silk shirt. It was open to his chest, where the Iron Cross dangled prominently.

He took out a cigarette and lit it and lazily sat back and looked over the place, his eyes cold and appraising. This was the fourth coffeehouse he had been to this night, and he was beginning to lose hope. The heavy rain was keeping them inside their rooms and apartments. His eyes circled the room and then rested on a little group of four. They were seated in a corner on the right side of the stage, and he thought vaguely that one of them looked familiar to him. Brian could only see the fellow's profile. Wavy. hair, a sharp nose and a long jaw. He put his hand up and lowered his glasses and took another look, a hard, searching look, and he trembled.

It could be him. It could be.

The name was Tod. That's what Donna called him at the party. She had left Brian to go over to speak to Tod. And then they had gone outside into the dark garden, and when she came back to Brian, there was a tight, drawn look on her face, and soon she made him leave with her. She spoke very little the rest of the night.

There was fear in her that night, Brian said to himself. Now as I look back, I am sure it was fear.

Of what?

Of the death that was to come to her?

Brian stared across the room, and yet he couldn't be sure it was Tod. He knew he'd have to get closer to the table. He was about to rise, but he checked himself.

Easy, he murmured, you've got to be slow and patient. Mrs. Fisher was right. Be slow and controlled at all times. Watch every move you make, Brian. Every word you say and how you say it. Use the drawl. But use it carefully and make it sound true.

If you have to wait, wait it out.

You're fighting for your life, Brian. Always remember that.

Always!

He sat back in his chair again and set the dark glasses securely over his eyes. He watched the smoke of his cigarette curl up in front of him, and he found himself thinking of Donna, of her lying on the couch as if sleeping and then the phone ringing, ringing and the voice saying, "Run, pigeon, run."

And he said to himself wearily, as he had done a hundred times over, if I could only come upon the man with that voice.

He's the key to it all.

He would tell me why it all happened. He would help me. He saved me once. Surely, he would do it again.

If I could only hear his voice again.

Just once more.

But Brian heard another voice.

"You an Aryan?"

He turned and looked up into the face of the cowboy, the cowboy from Ohio.

"I guess I am," Brian said.

And he saw the fringed leather jacket, the blond hair that swept down to the man's shoulder and the gold ring on his finger.

The ring shaped into the head of a serpent with the two tiny diamond eyes that glittered so coldly.

"You're a long way from home."

"I could be."

"A real long way."

"Anything to you?" Brian asked harshly.

"Nothing."

He doesn't recognize me, Brian said to himself. I'm positive of that. Mrs. Fisher was right. Yes, she was.

We're going to use misdirection, Mrs. Fisher had said, the law of misdirection, Brian. It's the tool of the accomplished magician, his basic premise. That's how he's able to fool you. He takes your mind, your attention, and makes it all focus on something else. On what he wants you to see. Not on the object that is in front of you.

And you're going to use the same technique.

You're going to make them look at the Iron Cross and your corn-silk blond hair and your smoked glasses and the rest of your Aryan getup, and they won't see the true object standing before them—Brian Cawley, fugitive. Brian Cawley, the pigeon. Instead they'll see a tough, cynical motorcyclist from the Coast. A pure nihilist, as they are.

You have another thing going for you, Brian. According to the newspapers and the news reports, you are hiding out in Newark. There's no reason on earth for you to be walking the streets of the Village. That's the last place you should be.

According to their thinking, and the thinking of the police.

So you just play the part of the hard-as-nails Aryan as we've worked it out together. Play it to the hilt, and you'll be safe.

"Mind if I sit down?"

"Go ahead."

And he remembered Curley sitting on the stoop and talking to him and then walking off. And all the time Donna was lying upstairs in her apartment.

Lying there dead.

"They call me Curley," he said.

Brian looked at the powerful, stocky figure with the cowboy hat and the cold blue eyes and a rage rose within him.

You're part of them, aren't you, Curley? You were sitting on the stoop to make sure that I was the pigeon who came to see Donna. And then you walked off, sure that I was going upstairs to step into the trap.

Into the pigeon cage.

Brian's hand clenched under the table. And then it slowly relaxed again.

"Glad to meet you," he said quietly.

But within he swore to himself, I'll get you for this, Curley. I'll get you and all of them, all of them. Revenge? I'll have my revenge. I'll have it!

And then he remembered Mrs. Fisher's admonishing words, and he closed his lips tight and sat there gazing coldly at the man.

"I didn't get your name," Curley said.

"I didn't give you any," Brian said.

"What is it?"

"None of your business."

85

"That's how some of you Aryans operate?"

"That's how some of us do," Brian said curtly.

Curley smiled and tilted his cowboy hat farther back on his head.

"I hear tell you're a tough outfit out there."

"I don't think you've heard anything, Curley," Brian said.

"You're tough."

"I could be," Brian said.

"What's your specialty? Karate? Kung Fu?"

"Tai Chi."

"No."

"Yes. Any good Tai Chi man can beat a karate kook."

"Never."

"Want to try it?"

"I'm black belt, fifth dan. That's about as high as you can get."

"I still say, want to try it?"

"Yes. You are tough," Curley said slowly and evenly. "You're a Frisco bunch, aren't you?"

"I said you don't know anything, Curley," Brian said contemptuously.

"It's Frisco, isn't it?"

Brian shook his head.

"The headquarters is Sausalito."

"That's across the bay from Frisco."

"It's still Sausalito," Brian said harshly.

"I'll give you the point," Curley said.

They were silent. Brian snuffed out his cigarette in the ashtray. He looked at Curley's ring, at the hard, glittering eyes of the serpent, and then up into his face.

"So you've been out there," he said quietly.

"Yep. I travel at times."

"For whom?"

"For myself."

Brian looked at him and wanted to say, It is an organization, isn't it? What position do you hold in it?

Recruiter?

Fingerman?

Executioner?

Or all three of them at different times, eh, Curley?

He heard Curley's voice.

"What are you doing East? I've never seen any of you Aryans East."

"I could be here on assignment."

He saw the man's eyes widen.

"You must rate pretty high to be sent out."

"I rate," Brian said.

Curley sat there studying him.

"Or I could be here on my own. Just for kicks."

"You'll find them here."

"Will I?"

The waitress came over and set the glass of cappuccino down on the table. The flame of the candle was reflected in the tall glass. The girl smiled pleasantly at Curley and turned to Brian.

"You can pay now if you want to."

"I want to," Brian said and grinned up at her.

He took out a roll of bills that Mrs. Fisher had drawn out of the bank for him. He slowly peeled off a five and handed it to the girl.

She counted out his change and gave it to him.

"I'll be coming around again," she said.

"I'll take care of you then."

"Will you?" she smiled.

"Sure I will."

"I'll be around."

"I'll be here," he said and watched her go off, an easy smile on his lips.

"That's a lot of money you're showing," Curley said.

And he remembered Mrs. Fisher's words: "Only show the money when you're absolutely certain that it will help you. Be very, very careful with it."

Brian turned lazily to him.

"So?"

"It's a little unhealthy doing it here in the Village."

"You mean it's dangerous."

"I could put it that way."

87

"I'm used to danger," Brian said. "That's how I got the money."

He sipped at his cappuccino and looked away from him to the table near the stage. The fellow he thought was Tod was laughing.

It sent an icy feeling through Brian.

It's got to be Tod, he said to himself grimly. Things are falling into place. In my favor for a change.

"I like your style," Curley said.

"What's that supposed to mean?"

"And I like the Iron Cross. More people wearing them and this country wouldn't be in the shape it's in."

"Who gives a damn what shape the country's in?" Brian said. "It's every man for himself, isn't it?"

"Especially when the ship's sinking."

"I didn't even know there was a ship."

"There is. And it's sinking. Down into the sunset."

"Then let it sink. I've got my own boat."

Curley took out a panatella, slowly peeled off the cellophane and then put the long narrow cigar between his thick lips. He carefully lit it with a wooden match, striking the flame on his broad fingernail, and then leaned back and puffed a tiny cloud of blue smoke.

"I like your style," he said. "And I don't often say that to anybody."

"So?"

"And I don't often make mistakes about people."

"I'll bet you don't," Brian said sardonically.

Curley's eyes were like blue bits of steel.

"I don't, Aryan."

Brian leaned back in his chair.

"You're making a mistake about me, Curley."

"Yes?"

"You think I like you, don't you?"

"I didn't say anything about that."

"I don't like you," Brian said coldly. "Your body stinks."

Curley laughed, a low, mirthless laugh.

"Doesn't cut no ice with me. I don't want you to like me. It's better that way."

"For what?"

Curley puffed at his cigar silently. Brian waited.

"What's your plans for the rest of the night, Aryan?"

"Why?"

"I'd like to spend more time with you and talk."

"About what?"

"About how you can make yourself another roll of bills to take back home with you."

"Doing what?"

Curley seemed to hesitate a split second, and then he spoke.

"Maybe doing something for us."

"Us?"

"That's what I said."

"Who's us, Curley?"

Curley pointed to the small corner table.

"Those are some friends of mine."

So it is Tod, Brian thought. And Donna's face came before him, and there was a dark look of terror in her eyes.

Be careful, Brian, the eyes seemed to plead, be careful.

He heard Curley's voice come to him as from a distance.

"We're going over to a loft to see a show. Want to come along?"

"What kind of a show?"

"Something you'll like."

"How do you know I will, Curley? You just met me."

"And sized you up and took a decision on you."

"And you make no mistakes."

"No mistakes. It's a thrill show."

"Oh?"

"You said you're here for kicks, didn't you?"

Brian nodded.

"I did."

"We like our kicks, too."

I'll bet you do, Brian thought grimly and glanced again at the corner table; I'll bet you do.

"What kind of a thrill show?" he asked.

Curley sat back and pursed his lips and sent up a ring of smoke. He watched it waft away into the dimness and slowly dissolve.

"A mongoose fighting a fer-de-lance," he said.

"What?"

Curley laughed.

"You think I'm putting you on, don't you?"

"A mongoose?"

"You never saw it, did you?"

Brian slowly shook his head.

"It's a great show. Something to tell the folks back home about."

"Sounds interesting."

"Want to come along?"

"What time does the show start?"

"In an hour or so. You can bet on the mongoose, or you can bet on the snake. You can take your pick. You can get good odds on the snake."

"But?"

"He almost always looses."

"I'll take the mongoose," Brian said. "I like a winner."

"Do you?"

But Curley wasn't listening to him anymore. He had turned away from Brian and was looking at the stage. And on the stage the guitar player had started a new song.

The words floated pure and clear to Brian. He felt a shiver go through him as he listened to them.

> Weep for Daddy-O
> O weep for Daddy-O
> You die once
> You die twice
> Just ain't no difference
> 'Cause dying once is forever
> 'Cause dying once is forever

The voice of Curley broke through to him. "A great song, isn't it?"

The singer on the stage was done. He reached down again for his beer bottle and drank again from it.

It seemed to Brian to be a never-emptying bottle. It will last the night away. It will last the world away.

It's as though I'm sitting here in a dream, he said to himself. In a nightmare world. In a room of flickering candlelights and shadows on bare walls and figures sitting at tables. Figures who will soon waver and dissolve into the dim air like Curley's smoke rings.

And Curley?

This killer who sits across the table from me with the cowboy hat and eyes that hate and dismiss everything.

It's all crap to you, isn't it, Curley?

The whole world. If you don't like it, why don't you do something about changing it? Not destroying it?

Killing other people.

Who in the hell ever gave you the right to destroy another human being? Who? Damn you, who!

"Ever hear that song before, Aryan?"

"No."

"When you die it's forever. You believe in an afterlife? In an afterworld?"

Curley's blue eyes seemed to be boring into him. The face was suddenly hard and piercing. The lips a thin line like a knife. It was the face of an executioner, Brian thought. He looked into the eyes without flinching and then turned to the candle on the table. He blew it out.

"That's what I believe in, Curley," he said. "Once the light is out it's all over."

Curley sat there looking at him. His face was shadowed.

"I like your style," he said. "You're coming to the show?"

"I've got to take care of something first."

"For Sausalito?"

"It could be."

"And then you'll come to the show?"

"I might be able to make it. I might need a little more time."

"Give yourself two hours. Show won't really be under way until then."

"Where is it?"

"Thirty-four Barton. Top floor."

"Thirty-four."

"Ring three times and then one short one."

"Okay."

"You'll be there, Aryan?"

"I'll try to."

"That's good enough for me."

Then he saw Curley rise and go over to the corner table and pull up a chair and join the group.

After a while, Brian got up and left the place.

16

He sat in the kitchen, eating with her. They had been silent a long while, each with their own sombre thoughts. She put down her fork, and it clattered on the plate. That was the only sound in the room. Outside the rain drove along the empty street.

Mrs. Fisher rose and went to the stove and picked up the coffeepot and then poured coffee into two cups and came back to the table and set one cup by him and one in her place.

She sat down again.

"It's a weird bunch," she said.

"Yes," he murmured.

"Weird and deadly."

"They're killers, all right," Brian said.

She put a teaspoon of sugar into her coffee. And then stirred it thoughtfully.

"The police?"

He shook his head.

"You know yourself the answer, Mrs. Fisher."

"I know, And yet. . . ."

"We've got nothing to go to them with. Nothing.

They'll only listen to me and then shove me into a cell."

"There's this Curley character and Tod and the rest of them."

"And nothing. Absolutely nothing to pin them with."

"How does your arm feel?"

"It's in pretty good shape."

She drank her coffee and spoke again.

"I wonder what he wants you to do for them?"

Brian shrugged.

"No idea."

"But you'll find out soon enough."

"Yes."

"When do you think you'll come back?"

"Anybody's guess."

"You'll leave me an address, Brian."

"All right."

"I don't like this," she said.

He looked across the table at her tight, haggard face.

"Is there any choice?"

"I don't like this," she said again, her voice becoming tense.

"But, Mrs. Fisher, you know that there is nothing we can. . . ."

She suddenly pushed the cup away from her, and the coffee spilled onto the white tablecloth, darkening it.

"No," she said. "No."

She rose and swung away from him and went to the front window and stared out into the night. Stood there and didn't say a word.

The rain gusted against the window. He sat at the table, his eyes focused on the darkening stain.

It reminded him of blood. Of the blood seeping from the wound in his arm after the bullet hit it.

"I should stop you from going, Brian. I should stop you," she said without turning to him, as if speaking to the darkness outside.

He didn't say anything.

"I've no right to let you risk your life this way."

"We've been through this before, Mrs. Fisher."

"I've no right," she said, not hearing him.

"There's nothing you can do. I'd go ahead anyway." She turned to him.

"A phone call to the police. That's all I have to do."

"No."

"Just a phone call, Brian. Why not?" she asked harshly.

"You wouldn't do it. Think of what it would mean to you, Mrs. Fisher."

"I know what it would mean to me."

"We're tied together. You yourself said that. I prove my innocence, and you're in the clear also. You'd be throwing away your chance to. . . ."

"Then I throw it away," she cut in. "I'll take what's coming to me."

"You can't do it," he said.

"I'm thinking of you, Brian."

"You're not."

"It is so, Brian."

He shook his head fiercely.

"You wouldn't talk this way," he said. "Not if you really cared for me."

"Cared?"

She stared at him and bit her lip as if to keep from crying out. She moved away from him and stood gazing out the window into the night.

"Not if you had any feeling for me," he said.

"You can say that?"

"Yes," he said brutally. "Because if you did you would never. . . ."

He stopped speaking for she had turned to him and he saw that there were tears in her eyes. Little, glistening tears.

"Brian Cawley."

"I—I didn't mean to hurt you," he said.

He couldn't look at her. He sat down in the chair, head averted.

"Brian Cawley," she said gently and went over to her chair and sat down on it.

The only sound was that of the ever-falling rain.

"Feeling for you?" she suddenly said in a low voice. "No feeling for you?"

He didn't speak.

"I've never had any children, Brian," she said. "You and all the others through the long years—you were my children. It sounds like an old, tired cliché, doesn't it? The spinster teacher letting out all her pent-up love on the children of her classes. The childless teacher doing the same. But it's true. True as the tears in my eyes."

"Mrs. Fisher," he said and he couldn't go on.

"Feeling for you? After what has happened to you? You question my feeling for you?"

"I—I didn't mean to say it."

"After your great loss? Your losing Donna?"

He bowed his head. Her soft, agonized words were like blows to him.

"You're young," she said tenderly. "And when you lose when you're young, then it hurts the most. I know that is true, Brian. How well I know it."

She got up and came over to him and stood there close, looking down at him.

"Brian," she said.

He slowly looked up at her.

"Brian, I shall tell you something I have never told anybody."

"Yes?"

The lights in her eyes had changed, and it seemed to him that they began to glow. Sadly. Poignantly.

"Brian," she said. "I lived with my husband twenty-five years. It was a good marriage. He was the best friend I ever had. But I never loved him."

He stared at her.

"No, Brian. Never. And although I never said a word to him, he knew the truth. The man I loved was killed in the war. Long before I met my husband. I never stopped loving him. Never, Brian. It will be with me to my last day."

"I didn't mean to hurt you," he murmured.

"So I know your feeling for Donna. I know it too well, Brian."

Her voice broke, and he saw her strong hands quiver.

After a while he got up from his chair, and he put on his leather jacket, his visored cap and his dark glasses. He took off Donna's locket, handed it to Mrs. Fisher, and he put on the Iron Cross.

"I'm going now," he said.

Then he went out and closed the door behind him, leaving her there alone.

17

It was while Curley was showing him the fer-de-lance and pointing out the little dark red triangles on the coiled body that he heard the voice.

"The snake comes from Martinique," the voice behind Brian said. "It is one of the most poisonous snakes in the world. Grows to a length of six feet or more."

"Sometimes eight feet," Curley said.

"That's true. Very true."

Brian turned to the speaker. It was Tod.

"Every year there are people who die in Martinique. Workers in the cane fields. Or people who just stroll in the forest areas. Killed by the fer-de-lance."

"Maybe over a hundred every year."

"I'd say about fifty, Curley."

"He looks pretty mean," Brian said.

"He is pretty mean."

"But he doesn't faze the mongoose," Curley laughed.

"He doesn't. Have you ever been to Martinique?"

"No," Brian said.

And he felt that Tod was studying and appraising him.

"It's beautiful. You should go there. Gave me a zing to hear black people speak cultivated French. Do you speak French?"

"No," Brian said.

"Been to college?"

"In and out."

"Which one?"

"I'd say that's my business. Wouldn't you?"

"Of course. I'm glad you came to our little show."

"Call him Aryan." Curley smiled.

"I shall." Tod smiled.

He put his hand out to Brian, and Brian shook it. Tod's grasp was firm and assured. He was slight, with brown thinning hair, a sharp intelligent face and a quiet well-modulated voice. He had the bearing of a young college instructor. Maybe he is, Brian thought. He was in his early or mid-twenties. He wore a dark-blue corduroy jacket and Levi's. He had small gold-rimmed glasses over his large brown eyes.

Shrewd cold eyes, Brian thought, even when they smiled.

"Curley is quite impressed with you, Aryan."

"Is he?"

"Yes. And Curley is an excellent judge of character."

"I get the idea he doesn't make mistakes."

"He doesn't."

"I've got a clean track record," Curley said, tipping his hat back.

"You have."

"No losses."

"Not up to now," Tod said.

It was said quietly and easily. Almost a murmur. Yet Brian felt a cold ripple of fear pass over him. And he saw again the dark look of terror on Donna's face as she came back out of the garden with Tod.

"Maybe he is making a mistake," he said curtly.

Tod smiled genially.

"Let us decide, Aryan."

They had moved away from the small platform and the wire-netted cages and now stood near the center of the room. There were old couches, easy chairs and some wooden folding chairs spread out over the entire space of the vast loft. It was one huge, sprawling living room. The ceiling was high and blue, with a sprinkling of large gold stars across its entire length. On the blue walls were framed reproductions of the French impressionists. A series of Lautrec posters with their dominant yellows lay on the far wall. And on the chairs and couches and in the areas about them were clusters of people in casual dress, talking and laughing pleasantly.

They were mostly young, of college age or just a bit older, Brian surmised.

And he was surprised at seeing them. He had expected a gathering of Village loners, kooks, and weirdos with their outlandish costumes. A fer-de-lance fighting it out with a mongoose. Who would come to see that but a bunch of kooks and weirdos?

Yet now it seemed to him that he had stumbled into a college party of a fairly conservative university. An old Ivy League one. Like Brown University in Provincetown. He had gone there once with Donna. And it had turned out to be a pretty stodgy affair.

He estimated there were at least fifty people in the loft. And as he surveyed them more closely, he began to see a scattering of weirdo outfits among them. It made him feel more at ease in his Aryan getup. He would blend in.

A bar had been set up at one end of the room, and people were buying drinks and lounging about it and talking.

"How do you like the turnout, Aryan?" Curley asked.

"Looks pretty good. You always get one like this?"

"For our special shows," Tod answered. "Always."

"Thrills bring them in," Curley said.

"It's a thrill world," a resonant, mellow voice said.

"A thrill world and a bloody world. People are killed every day—for thrills."

Brian turned and saw a tall, reddish-haired fellow join them. He wore a light-grey jacket, grey pants and black shoes that had a sheen to them. He had a narrow, pointed reddish beard. His face was rugged and his features large.

His eyes were grey and twinkling.

"People enjoy death," he said. "Seeing it done to others. Or even to themselves. Don't you think so?"

"I guess they do," Brian said.

"I'm Rolfe. *R-o-l-f-e.*"

"This is Aryan," Tod said to him.

"Yes. Curley's been telling me about you."

"I have," Curley said.

"Curley sure does a lot of talking, doesn't he?" Brian smiled.

Rolfe laughed. It was a warm, pleasant-sounding laugh.

"For a cowboy, yes. They're supposed to be the silent taciturn type. At least that's what the movies tell us. You going back to the Coast soon?"

"In a while," Brian said.

"How are things out there? Anybody dying?"

Brian looked into the twinkling eyes and tried to search out what was behind them. This Rolfe is pretty cool and dangerous, he thought.

And then he said to himself, Christ, they're all pretty cool and dangerous. With a touch of madness.

"There's always somebody dying out there," he said.

And that touch of madness makes them even more dangerous.

"Violently?"

"I'd say so."

"There's always somebody dying out here," Rolfe said. "Violently."

"How very true," a woman said.

She was tall and dressed in a deerskin Indian costume, fringed with blue-and-white tiny beads. She had Navaho silver bracelets on both her long wrists. And she wore a large silver shell necklace that hung down to her waist.

Her hair was honey-blond and parted in the middle.

"Looks like a good evening," she said.

"It's night," Tod murmured.

"How true. The evening is gone. Night is upon us. Deep, desolate night."

"This is Marian," Tod said to Brian.

She turned to Brian and smiled at him. Her eyes were large and clear.

"You're Aryan," she said, her hand casually lifting the Iron Cross from his chest. "Aryan, Marian. We should make beautiful poetry together."

She let the Iron Cross drop back onto his chest again.

"Maybe we will," Brian smiled.

"You believe in astrology?"

"When I'm in trouble."

"Only then?"

"Only then."

"Are you in trouble now?"

"I could be," Brian laughed softly.

"Why do you think so?"

It was interesting to him that none of the others spoke. Just let her talk while they stood by listening. Listening to every word.

"Aren't we all in trouble these days?" Brian asked.

"All of us?"

"All of us."

"These days?"

"Exactly."

"So what does one do?"

He peered through his dark glasses at her. His face was white and taut.

"Sometimes you kill, I guess."

"Sometimes you kill," she repeated softly.

"That's what I said."

She looked from him to the others in the group, and their eyes seemed to meet and flash signals to each other.

"These are bad days, aren't they?" Rolfe asked.

"They are," Brian said.

"And when one kills, one is always paid," Tod said, his voice almost a whisper.

"Always."

"And the price?"

"Can be arranged," Brian said.

"I'm sure it can," Rolfe smiled.

"In old dollar bills. Unmarked."

"They're always old. And they're always unmarked."

"I like the Iron Cross," Marian said.

"I like it, too. That's why I wear it."

"I'll buy it from you."

"It's not for sale."

"But it will go so well with my Navaho outfit."

Will it? Brian said to himself grimly. And he thought of Mrs. Fisher and her love for the Navaho people.

"Well, Aryan?"

"I'll think it over, Marian." Brian smiled.

And it seemed to him, in the midst of the noise and the chatter of voices and the sound of the low music coming from the record player near the bar, that he was alone with this little group.

Virtually surrounded by them.

That they were holding a meeting then and there and coming to a judgment about him. He could see all this in Rolfe's twinkling grey eyes. Grey and deadly.

In Tod's quiet cool surveillance.

And in Marian's seeming absurdity.

Curley? Curley appeared to drift back, playing the silent observer. And Brian wondered who was the leader of the group.

It could be Rolfe or Tod.

And then he said to himself, It could be that Tod is the head out here. And that Rolfe has been sent in from abroad.

Maybe he is from one of the Scandinavian countries. There was something in the timbre of his voice and the way he pronounced certain words that seemed to indicate that he . . .

Or could it be Germany?

West Germany?

The Badder-Meinhof group of young terrorists was from West Germany. They were now in other countries, true. But Donna had said, West Germany.

He remembered Donna speaking about terrorists and their appeal to the young of today. He was lying with her on the beach in Asbury Park. The blazing sun gave her hair a golden sheen, her lips glistened; he bent over to kiss her but she began to talk about terrorists and he wondered why she was doing it and then just as suddenly as she had begun it so she had cut it off. They were silent. They lay on the beach, a deserted part of the beach; the waves were laced with glittering foam, and he held her in his arms and kissed her.

But now as he looked back, back through a sad and grim perspective, he could see that she had wanted to tell him all she knew. And then for some inner reason decided not to.

And lost her life because of it.

"Want a drink?" Curley said to him.

"What?"

"A drink, Aryan."

"Oh, sure."

"Let's go over to the bar and get one."

"Why don't you two do that?" Rolfe said.

"Take care of him, Curley." Tod smiled.

"I will. Come on, Aryan."

"Okay," Brian said.

He nodded to them and followed Curley to the bar, and all the time he was sure of their eyes on his back.

Curley was taking him out of the meeting, and now they were going to vote on him. To come to a decision on whether he was safe to deal with or not. And whether he could do the job they wanted him to do.

"What'll it be, Aryan?"

"A vodka tonic," Brian said.

"Good choice," Curley said. "I'll have one, too."

"You like my style, Curley." Brian grinned.

"I do. All the way, Aryan."

They were silent while the bartender made their drinks. There was a little stir in the crowd as someone came in carrying a small wooden crate and made his way to the platform which held the cages.

"Jo-Jo and the mongoose," Curley said.

The fellow set the crate down, opened the door of the large empty cage and then let the mongoose go from the crate and into the cage. He slammed the door of the cage shut. The fer-de-lance lay coiled in its own small cage.

"He'll take the snake out and then put it in with the mongoose. And then the action will start," Curley said.

"And the odds?"

"Five to one, favoring the mongoose. But I'm taking the snake this time."

"Why?"

"A hunch. I always play hunches."

"Like with me," Brian said.

"Like with you, Aryan," Curley said quietly.

Brian turned away to take his drink.

"Here's to," Curley said and raised his glass.

"To what?"

"To life. A great big bunch of nothing."

"I'll buy that."

"To nothing."

There was a desolate poignant look in Curley's eyes. And then it faded out. They drank and lounged against the bar. Brian glanced toward the platform, but the fellow who had brought in the wooden crate was no longer standing there.

The mongoose moved restlessly in his cage. The snake raised its narrow lancelike head, slowly, sinuously.

"How do you like my friends?"

Brian turned back to Curley.

"They look interesting to me."

"They are, Aryan. They are interesting people."

"Have I met them all?"

Curley shook his head.

"Only the important ones, the wheels. There's one more left."

"Who's he?"

"The guy who brought in the mongoose."

"Oh."

"He's around somewhere."

"I'm here, Curley."

And Brian froze as he heard the voice. He almost dropped the glass from his hand. He slowly, deliberately, turned and faced the speaker.

"This is Jo-Jo," Curley said.

"And this is Aryan," Jo-Jo said.

He was short and swarthy and wiry. His eyes were black and piercing, like the eyes of a fierce and hungry hawk. His face small with high cheekbones. His hair was black like coal, and it shone dully. He had on a dark-blue shirt and grey pants. Around his small neck was a blue polka-dot bandana.

He wore a small gold earring that glimmered when the light caught it.

"Jo-Jo, the gypsy man," Curley said.

"I was born a gypsy, and I shall die one." Jo-Jo smiled. His voice had a metallic tone.

"You'll live a long time," Curley said. "Gypsies live forever."

"And cowboys."

"They die, Jo-Jo. They die in the sunset. Did you bring us a good mongoose this time?"

"A real killer. Smuggled off a freighter in from Grenada."

Curley turned to Brian.

"He's the greatest. You give him an assignment, and he never fails. Do you, Jo-Jo?"

"Never."

"Then I shouldn't put my money on the fer-de-lance?"

"I wouldn't. The fer-de-lance has no chance."

Jo-Jo laughed, a low metallic laugh, and as he did

so, Brian wanted to shout to him, I am the pigeon, the pigeon. And you are the voice that saved my life.

"How soon till the show gets underway?" Curley asked.

"That's up to Tod. Can get started now if he wants. You'd better collect the bets."

"I'll go over and talk to him. You keep Aryan company."

"Whatever you say, Curley."

They watched Curley make his way back to the little group. From where he stood, Brian could see that they were still talking seriously.

Concentrated upon each other.

He turned back to the gypsy and spoke.

"I've heard your voice before."

"Have you?"

"Yes," Brian said. "I'm sure of it."

"What are you drinking?

"A vodka tonic.

"I think I'll have a white wine. Do you mind?"

"Not at all."

He watched the gypsy order his drink, and he looked again at the group. Curley had now joined them and he was speaking to Tod.

Jo-Jo held the wine glass in his hand. He jiggled it a bit and watched the amber liquid stir and then become quiet again.

"Where was it, Aryan?" he asked quietly.

Brian drank a little more before answering.

"On a telephone."

And he saw the black eyes narrow. That was the only change of expression in the man's face.

"You called me a pigeon," Brian said.

Jo-Jo put the glass of wine to his lips and drank a bit, savoring it, slowly, ever so slowly, and then he set the glass down and looked at the bar, his face averted.

"Don't make a bad move," he said. "Or we're both dead. Is that clear to you? Be casual."

"I will."

"You're just shooting the breeze with me."

"Sure."

He swung around to Brian and laughed.

"They're more dangerous than that fer-de-lance over there."

"I know." Brian smiled.

"They find you out and you are. . . ." He didn't finish the sentence.

"They haven't up to now."

"Let's keep it that way. Now listen to me. Meet me at Thirteen Gary Street. A cellar apartment. At four o'clock."

"This morning?"

"Yes. It will still be dark out. So be careful that you're not followed. Be very careful."

"I'll be there."

"And now drink again and smile because Curley is coming back."

Brian smiled and raised the glass to his lips.

"And that's how I fell off the motorcycle," Jo-Jo said.

"You can't ride eighty miles an hour drunk and stay on a bike."

"That's what the hospital interne said." Jo-Jo laughed.

"You like his style, Jo-Jo?"

"I do, Curley. We talk the same language."

Curley grinned at Brian and turned back to the gypsy.

"Tod says let's get on with the show. I'll go around to collect the bets. You can get the two fighters ready to go."

"Okay, Curley."

"I'm still betting on the fer-de-lance. How about you, Aryan?"

"I'll play your hunch. Put me down for fifty."

Curley smiled. "Going along with old Curley, eh?"

"Even if I lose."

"You'll win, Aryan. Anybody follows old Curley has to win. That right, Jo-Jo?"

But the gypsy was not with them anymore. He had gone to the cages.

"He moves fast," Curley said.

"He does."

Curley took out one of his thin cigars, removed the cellophane and then lit one of his wooden matches with the nail of his thick finger. He puffed.

"I've never trusted a gypsy."

"Why not?"

"They all move too fast."

"Nothing wrong in that."

Curley pursed his lips and watched a ring of smoke waft up. "Too shifty."

"You say you've never trusted a gypsy. And yet . . . ?"

"Jo-Jo? He's all right. He's come through."

"I'll put my money on Jo-Jo. From what I've seen of him," Brian said.

Curley's eyes suddenly clouded. "Would you?" he asked softly.

And Brian somehow felt that he had spoken too much. He didn't answer Curley.

"I'll collect the bets," Curley said and walked off.

Brian looked toward the little group, but it was no longer there. Its members were now moving around among the crowd of guests.

He wondered what their decision was. And then he found out.

It was when the mongoose closed his jaws over the darting head of the fer-de-lance, and the crowd began to shout and Brian wondered who were the animals and who the humans, that Curley said: "You've been voted in, Aryan. And somebody's been voted out."

"Who is it?"

"I'll tell you tomorrow."

"Okay with me," Brian said.

"Meet me here at three in the afternoon."

"Check."

"Check," Curley said. "You've lost fifty dollars."

And then he walked away from him.

18

___

He waited, flattened against the cold wall of the building, until the prowl car passed up the dark street, and then he moved quickly back to the sidewalk and hurried down the block till he came to number 13. He went down a short flight of stone steps and paused in a well of darkness. He looked at the glowing dial of his watch. It showed two minutes to four.

He groped along till he saw the faint gleam of a brass doorknob and then the form of an old wooden door. He knocked softly a few times. He waited. Then he knocked again.

This time the door opened.

"Come in."

He went in, and the door closed swiftly and silently behind him.

"Follow me."

He saw in the harsh beam of the searchlight the grey bulk of a boiler, and then they passed it and came to a small room in the back of the cellar. The door was open.

"In here."

The gypsy closed the door and the light of the flashlight went out, and for an instant, a terrifying instant, Brian stood in complete darkness and wondered if he had walked into a fatal trap. His hands began to shake.

An overhead bulb suddenly lit the darkness.

"Sit over there."

He saw an old couch and two dusty armchairs. There were dark-green shades over the two narrow windows that looked out on a small yard.

Brian sat down on one of the chairs.

The walls of the room were bare, grey and shadowy. Jo-Jo was sitting quietly on the couch, and it was only then, as he looked at him, that Brian saw the revolver at his side. It lay a few inches away from his right hand.

You can't trust gypsies, Curley had said.

"Tell me about yourself."

And gypsies don't trust you.

"I'm Brian Cawley."

"Go on."

The silence about them was heavy and impenetrable. And it came to Brian that no one would ever hear the shot if Jo-Jo were to fire that gun.

They could just as well be sitting in an iron vault.

"Your phone call saved me from the police. And jail."

"And who took the bullet out of you?"

"An old teacher of mine. She believes in my innocence."

Jo-Jo sat gazing at him, his face smooth and impassive. The light glinted off his coal-black hair.

"And this Aryan getup?"

"Was her idea. I wanted to . . ."

The gypsy cut in softly. "You wanted to find out who killed Donna?"

"Yes."

"And why you were set up as a pigeon?"

"I know why."

"And who made the phone call? Find the man and he'll prove you innocent."

"I'm looking at that man," Brian said.

111

Jo-Jo smiled, a sardonic smile.

"You've been doing pretty well up to now, Brian."

"Up to now?"

And Brian felt a cold shiver go through him.

"I can't help you prove your innocence."

"What do you mean?"

"I made a mistake in trying to save you from being a pigeon."

"Why? Tell me why?"

But the gypsy didn't answer. He stared at Brian for a long while. There seemed to be an almost eternal sadness deep in his black eyes.

Finally he spoke. "I'm an undercover man, Brian. For one of the federal agencies. My trying to help you put me and the entire project in danger. That's why I say it was a mistake."

Brian was silent.

"The last man sent in to infiltrate this terrorist organization was found on a Long Island beach. Washed up from the ocean. Six bullets in his body."

His voice had tensed, and suddenly he got up with a swift, sharp motion and came over to Brian.

"Take off that damned thing you're wearing. I can't stand to look at it. I'm a gypsy, and the Nazis went out of their way to murder my people. Take it off."

His eyes glowed.

"I don't like it either," Brian said, and he lifted the Iron Cross up and over his head and then put it into his pants pocket.

Jo-Jo's face softened.

"I can't help you now to prove your innocence, Brian. It's too damned dangerous. There's too much at stake."

"I understand," Brian said. But within he felt desolate and empty.

"This is a sick outfit we're dealing with," Jo-Jo said in a low and controlled voice. "I've been able to penetrate the outer ring. But never the inner one. I learned that Donna was to be voted out. But I didn't know

112

when she was going to be executed. I found out too late to save her."

"Who killed her?"

"Our resident Navaho."

"Marian?"

"Yes. She won Donna's confidence and then betrayed her. She was in the apartment when Donna called you to come and see her."

Brian bowed his head and clenched his hands till the nails almost cut into the skin.

"And who knocked me out and poured the whiskey over me? Put the knife in my hand?"

"Rolfe."

"Why was she killed?" he asked in a low and tortured voice.

"The Saturday plan."

Brian slowly raised his head.

"What?"

"Tod was in love with her. He told her about the Saturday plan. It was too much for her to live with. She wanted out. They killed her."

"What is the Saturday plan?"

"A plan to kill many people at one time. That's all we know."

Brian stared at him.

"This is an international organization of terrorists, Brian. We have one of their top leaders in jail here. We've kept this very quiet. Out of the press. We want to extradite him to West Germany to stand trial for murder. The organization wants him released and flown out of the country to freedom. Or else. . . ."

He paused and went on.

"This Saturday at two-thirty in the afternoon there will be a disaster in this city. Where it will be, they don't say. A lot of time bombs will go off. I can tell you that. All in one place."

"And if you don't release him? Even after that?"

"There'll be more Saturday plans—until we do."

"You can't stop them?"

Jo-Jo shook his head.

"Not up to now. We're closing in on them. But we have no concrete evidence yet. Our main concern now is to stop the Saturday plan."

"Do you think they suspect you?"

Jo-Jo's small wiry hand stroked his hair again and again, and then he spoke.

"They've been wondering how you escaped the set-up, who tipped you off. Wondering and doing a lot of quiet questioning. It was a damn fool thing I did. I disobeyed my orders and obeyed an instinct, a human feeling."

He sighed softly. "I might have to pay for it."

"No," Brian said.

Jo-Jo smiled sadly at him.

"I believe I'd do it again, Brian. If I had to."

Brian looked at him and couldn't speak.

"We're trained and we're trained and we're trained," Jo-Jo said. "And then you find out, you're still a human being. You can't train that out."

He smiled again, and then his face hardened.

"What did Curley tell you tonight?"

"He said I've been voted in. I'm to get the assignment tomorrow."

"And?"

Brian drew a deep breath, and then he spoke.

"He said somebody's been voted out."

The gypsy's eyes flashed, but he was silent.

"The assignment is for me to kill somebody."

"I know."

Brian leaned forward to him, an agonized pleading look on his face.

"What should I do, Jo-Jo? I'm starting to get scared. Awfully scared."

"First thing is don't panic."

"I'm trying not to."

"You see Curley, and then you call me at this number." He wrote it on a slip of paper and handed it to Brian. "I'll tell you what to do."

"All right," Brian said and he began to feel calmer. He put the slip of paper into his pocket.

"Now remember you're not to tell anybody about me."

"Not even Mrs. Fisher?"

"Mrs. Fisher?"

"The teacher who—"

"No," Jo-Jo cut in harshly. "Nobody, I say. And stay away from the police."

"The police?" Why should I want to . . .?"

"You might be getting some ideas. To go to them with information about Curley and the rest. Don't. We've got to stop the Saturday plan. We've got to break up this outfit for good. Going to the police now would ruin everything."

"I wasn't going to the police," Brian said curtly.

"All right then. We understand each other."

"I'm in this all the way, Jo-Jo," Brian said fiercely. "Just as you are."

The gypsy looked at him and smiled, his sad slow smile.

"All the way, Brian," he murmured softly.

He got up.

"Put on that Iron Cross again. And get out of here."

"Okay," Brian said.

"And be careful, Brian. For your sake. And mine."

"I will, Jo-Jo," he said.

And Brian never forgot the last words the gypsy spoke to him, just before he opened the door to let him out into the dying night. He had turned off the flashlight, and the darkness was about them, deep and impenetrable.

Brian never forgot the glowing, ancient eyes. The glimmer of the gold earring. Nor the low, flowing voice that was rich with feeling.

"Hold my hand, Brian, and let me speak to you as brother to brother. My true name is Aram. I'm a graduate of Wisconsin University—master's from Columbia—Political Science. I feel close to you, Brian. Do you know why? I feel that you have faith. I know this is in you. Man will make it, won't he? He'll build a better world for himself. And your generation will help do it,

115

Brian. I'm not talking about the Curleys, the Tods, the Rolfes, the Marians. I'm talking about the Brian Cawleys, the Donna Madisons and all the rest of you. You'll bring about a change, a deep and far-reaching change. And you'll banish the atom bomb to the moon."

He paused and then said slowly and gravely, "Take care, Brian."

"Good-bye, Aram," Brian said.

And then he left him.

19

When he got back to Mrs. Fisher's apartment, she was sitting in her chair, head bowed, asleep. The thin light of morning was coming through the window. He waked her gently and then told her what had happened. But he didn't say a word about the gypsy.

Not a single word.

She sat there silent and thoughtful for a long while. A motionless, brooding figure. There was grey clay on her hands, and he knew that she had been working on her sculpture. Trying to keep her mind off her great anxiety for him.

He felt a great and tender melancholy sweep over him as he looked at her hands. And then up at her tired and haggard face.

She began to speak.

"After you see that hideous Curley and find out what the assignment definitely is, you come back here, Brian."

"Here?"

He saw her jaw harden.

"Is that clear to you, Brian? Here."

He nodded silently.

"And this time we're going to the police. This time for sure. And you'll tell them all that you know."

He thought of Jo-Jo and what he had said to him.

You are not to go to the police. You'll ruin everything.

"Well, Brian?"

We must stop the Saturday plan. One way or another, Brian. Many lives are at stake.

"Brian."

He gazed at her silently.

"Brian," she said again.

"What?"

She got up and came over to his chair. Her voice lashed out at him.

"Brian, as God is my witness, I'll go there myself right now if you don't agree to what I say."

"All right," he said gently. "I'll come back here, and we'll go to the police."

And he hated himself for lying to her.

118

20

"What we want done, we want done tonight," Curley said.

"Why tonight?" Brian asked. "What's the hurry?"

"Because tonight is Friday. We have some plans for tomorrow, Aryan. We want this cleared away."

"Then it'll be tonight."

Curley took out an envelope and held it in his hand.

"There's seven hundred and fifty dollars in here."

"Only seven fifty?"

"Seven hundred and fifty when you deliver."

They were leaning on the long bar. The cages were still on the platform. But they were empty.

Only he and Curley were in the loft.

"You don't mind what time it happens tonight?"

"Pick your own."

"Okay. And what is it you want delivered?"

Curley swished the amber liquid in his glass and then drank and put down the glass.

"Death."

Brian whitened.

"I see."

"You understood that all along, didn't you, Aryan?"

"I guess I did."

"We want it done cleanly."

"I've done it that way before."

"That's what I figured."

"I leave no traces, Curley."

"Good. And then we want you to leave town and go on back home."

"Those are my plans."

"There's a morning plane out from Kennedy. To Frisco."

"And you want me on it?"

"We'll give you the ticket when we give you the rest of the money."

"And my bike?"

"Take it right with you."

Brian smiled.

"Everything's fine with me."

Curley grinned.

"So what's to argue?"

"I don't see any arguing."

"Good. We wanted this done by an outsider because the person voted out will be caught by surprise. In case you're wondering."

"I wasn't. That's how the mobsters generally do it. For top people."

"This one's not so top. But he was getting close."

Brian waited.

"We were looking for an outsider, and you came along just at the right time, Aryan."

Brian lifted his glass and let a cube of cooling ice slip into his mouth.

"And who is it?"

"The surprise victim?"

"Yes."

"The gypsy."

He felt Curley's eyes bore into him, like bits of cold blue steel.

"You never trusted a gypsy. Did you, Curley?"

"Never. Nor do my friends anymore."

"And where do I find him?"

120

"You don't have to."

"What do you mean?"

"We're coming here at ten for a little meeting. Concerning our plans for tomorrow. You can take him after we all drift away."

Brian glanced at the two empty desolate cages.

"How do you know he'll be here, Curley?"

"One of us will go to his apartment and pick him up. Jo-Jo lives like a little prince in a beautiful apartment on Waverly Place. Doorman and all."

"Waverly Place?"

"Uh-huh. Jo-Jo has a rich father in the Midwest who keeps him in money. A spice merchant. He won't need him anymore after tonight. Will he, Aryan?"

"What time do you want me here tonight?" Brian asked coldly.

"Just before ten."

"I'll show up."

"I know you will. Do a clean job. We'll take care of the body."

Brian silently set down his glass.

"Never trust a gypsy," Curley said.

And then he drank.

21

He heard Jo-Jo's metallic voice. "Make it short."

"You've been voted out."

"So it is me," he said.

"I'm to do it after tonight's meeting at the loft."

"The meeting's set for ten o'clock."

"That's what he said. Somebody's going to your apartment. To pick you up. To make sure that you go to it."

There was a silence.

Brian leaned against the glass wall of the phone booth and looked out at the grey and sombre day.

The booth was an isolated one on a quiet tree-shaded street. He had made sure that no one saw him go into it.

Few people passed up and down the block at this hour.

He waited for the gypsy to speak.

And he found himself thinking of the empty cages and of the single curving tooth of the fer-de-lance lying on the dull tin floor of one of them.

Lying white and stark.

While Curley spoke of death.

"What do you want me to do, Jo-Jo?" he asked, and his voice trembled.

"Easy, Brian. Easy. I'm thinking this out."

He waited, and then he heard the gypsy's voice again.

"Meet me at the hideout at eight. And we'll talk."

"All right. I'll be there."

"Be careful."

"I will."

He heard a click and he put down the phone, and as he stepped out of the booth, he almost walked into Tod.

"Aryan."

Brian felt a tremor go through him as he looked at the slight and genial man.

"Hello, Tod," he said.

"Just making a call?"

"Yes."

He had come from nowhere. It was almost eerie, as if he had been part of one of the leafy trees and suddenly. . . .

Brian felt a tightening in his chest.

"Anything important?"

"That's my business, isn't it?"

Tod smiled, his eyes twinkled behind his gold-rimmed glasses. He leaned casually against the wide trunk of an old plane tree. His two hands lay deep in his pockets.

"Of course, it is," he said pleasantly. "I'm merely making conversation."

Are you? Brian thought grimly. What is going on in that fine brain of yours? That arrogant twisted brain?

"Did you see Curley?"

"Yes."

"And?"

And you loved Donna? You?

"Everything's fine," Brian said.

"All settled?"

"Yes."

"And you are satisfied?"

123

"Perfectly."

Tod smiled and looked easily about him. "This is a pleasant block, isn't it? One of my favorites in the Village."

"I like it."

To love Donna and then to kill her and yet to call yourself a human being. While your eyes still smile and smile, and that ruthless brain of yours ticks on and on —like a time bomb.

"You have a room in this area?"

Brian shook his head.

"No. I'm staying at one of the Ys uptown."

"Good idea."

"Why is it a good idea?"

Tod shrugged.

"Well, for one thing one can become anonymous in a Y. You can slip in and out, and no one ever knows the difference. Who really cares or notices? Isn't that so?"

"There is something in that," Brian said.

"Of course there is. And that's why you're staying there, Aryan. You know your way around, don't you?"

"Maybe I do."

"You're a survivor."

"It's a hard world we've made for ourselves."

Tod's eyes glinted. The smile was gone—wiped out.

"We? Or our damn fool elders? Our bloated, pointed-headed fathers. Our fat-assed mothers. These bastards robbed us of a world. Why not strike back at them? Scare the hell out of them. Destroy everything they hold sacred. Spit at their idols. Blow up their institutions. Why not?"

And then he was smiling easily again.

"I guess that's what I mean," Brian said.

Tod chuckled softly and held out his hand.

"See you tonight, Aryan."

Brian shook Tod's hand, and it was cold and damp to the touch.

"Sure thing, Tod," he said.

He watched Tod walk up the block till he was out of

124

sight. And a feeling went through him that something was wrong.

Desperately wrong.

Brian was about to step back into the booth and call the gypsy, and then he quickly changed his mind.

It's only a feeling. I'll see him in a few hours and tell him then.

Brian never forgave himself for that decision.

22

He had once read in a Joseph Conrad tale that a lie corrodes the liar. And he felt that bitter corrosion within him as he phoned Mrs. Fisher and told her that Curley had held him off.

"What do you mean, Brian?"

"It's set, and it's not set."

"You're talking riddles," she said sharply.

"They're having a little meeting tonight. They want me there. To go over things."

"What time?"

"About eight or so."

"Then come back here. I want to see you."

He hesitated.

"I'm in the coffeehouse with Curley."

"So?"

"He wants me to pass the time with him until the meeting."

"Can't you get out of it?"

"I don't see how. Not without raising his suspicions."

He could see her holding the phone and thinking. Her face tight and anxious. He spoke again.

"Everything's going along fine, Mrs. Fisher. I don't

think I ought to do anything to. . . ." His voice trailed away into silence.

"He said nothing about the assignment?"

"Just that it's set for tomorrow."

"Tomorrow?"

There was a tone of relief in her voice.

"Yes."

"Brian."

"Yes, Mrs. Fisher?"

He was waiting for her to say, are you telling me the truth? Are you? But then he thought to himself, she believes in me so thoroughly, so completely. She would never think that I would lie to her. Not after all she's done for me.

He heard her voice.

"Try to get back here as soon as you can."

"I will."

"Please," she said.

He felt the world of anxiety and emotion that was in the word, felt it to his core.

"I'm okay. I'm really okay," he said.

He put his hand to his eyes.

23

It had begun to rain, a hard, driving rain. And then there was thunder, low and rumbling. He was wet through and through when he came to the short flight of stone steps. He stood for an instant, eyes wary and piercing, and a flash of lightning illuminated him. The Iron Cross gleamed white and fiery, and then all was dark again.

Dark and silent.

Only the sound of the incessant rain, a brooding sound.

Brian went down the steps and then groped his way along the wall till he saw the glint of the doorknob. He stopped by it, and there was another peal of thunder and soon a flash of jagged lightning swept fiercely down from the street above and into his darkness, and just before it was blotted out, he saw that the door was partly open.

A shiver went through him.

He stood there hesitant and fearful, and then he put his hand forward till it felt the wet wood, and he quietly, delicately pushed the door open just a bit more. He leaned against the jamb and listened.

There was no sound from within.

Brian bent forward, his eyes straining into the darkness, and it was then that he saw the pencil thread of light coming from the back room.

He hesitated again and then stepped forward silently in the direction of the light. He took off his wide leather belt with its large brass buckle, and he slowly, deliberately, wrapped it around his clenched fist. He moved stealthily toward the thread of light, and when he came to the boiler room, the tip of his boot touched something, and he thought with horror of the fer-delance, alive and coiled.

He stood there tight and rigid and then peered down into the gloom, and he saw the legs and then the form of a sprawled body. And then close to the body, the dim outlines of a cowboy hat lying on the dusty stone floor.

Brian gasped and then went forward again to the thread of light. He came to it and then tentatively pushed the door open, and the glare of the overhead bulb was full upon him, and he saw the gypsy sitting on the couch, his head back, his eyes closed.

His gun lay locked in his right hand. The other hand was open and slack.

"Jo-Jo," Brian whispered.

There was a hole in his chest, and the blood was trickling from it.

"Jo-Jo," Brian cried out.

The eyes slowly opened and then focused, the sad, black eyes.

"Brian?"

Brian went quickly to him and knelt on the couch and put his arm gently about the gypsy's head. The hair was dark and moist.

"I'll get you help. I'll. . . ."

But the man shook his head weakly. "No. Too late," he murmured. "Too late."

"But . . ."

"Just listen."

His eyes closed again and then opened. Little beads

of perspiration were on his dark brow, glistening and gemlike.

Gypsy diamonds, Brian thought.

It was a wild, grotesque thought that flashed through him, and when it was gone, he felt like weeping.

"They found us out, Brian."

The voice was slow, and each word, each low word, was clear.

"When? I don't know. But Curley got in here and waited for me. To kill us both. He almost did. But I tricked him, a gypsy trick."

Brian had stopped listening.

"I'll get you to a doctor. Please let me . . ."

But the head shook grimly.

"Listen. The others might come soon. Tod, Rolfe. Call this number when you leave here. Call it and then tell them no . . . no Saturday plan. . . it's . . . to-night . . ."

A sudden paroxysm of coughing stopped him from speaking. Brian held him up tenderly, and soon the coughing ceased.

A pallor had come over the man's face, grey and frightening.

"Brian."

"Yes?"

"Remember . . . the number—"

Brian leaned closer to him. The man's voice had become weaker.

"What is it?"

"Stop them, Brian . . . stop—them . . . not—much time . . . they tricked . . . us . . ."

"Jo-Jo."

Suddenly the eyes opened wide, and a strange glow came into them.

"Brian?"

"Yes?"

His hands had begun to tremble. He stared at Brian and didn't seem to see him.

"Curley . . . time—table—"

"But . . ."

"Get it—in his—pocket . . ."

Brian looked anxiously at him.

"Jo-Jo, I . . ."

"Do it now . . . bombs in time . . . table . . . now . . ."

The eyes pleaded desperately with Brian. Brian got up and went quickly into the boiler room. He pulled the light cord violently, and the bulb swung back and forth, flinging harsh light and huge shadows over the grey, dusty walls. Brian stared at the sprawled figure, the open slack mouth, the eyes still wide with fear and surprise. He knelt and put his hand into one of the pockets of the deerskin jacket.

Far in the distance, in the muffled distance, he heard the sound of the rain, brooding and unceasing.

It was in the other pocket of the fringed jacket that he found the folded timetable. He didn't pause to examine it but gripped it tightly in his hand and hurried back to the gypsy.

"I have it," he said.

But the eyes were closed.

"Aram," Brian whispered.

And he knew there would be no answer.

24

He looked at the timetable under the lamplight, and he saw with a sinking heart what the gypsy meant when he said there was no Saturday plan.

"It's tonight. Tonight at nine," he said out loud.

He rushed out of the glare and into the darkness of the rainswept street searching with desperation for a cab. And all the time he thought of Curley lying against the boiler with the timetable in his pocket.

The fateful timetable—for the Staten Island Ferry.

He must've shown it to Jo-Jo when he had the drop on him. Shown it to him and laughed. Laughed at how they had tricked everybody. There is no Saturday plan, Jo-Jo. It's set for tonight just as your execution is.

The bombs are already planted. And they'll go off on the nine o'clock ferry. Sometime during its run from the Battery to Staten Island.

Look, you fool. I've underlined the time. See? Nine o'clock.

Brian glanced again at his watch. Only twenty-five minutes left. He turned and ran toward the subway station at Houston Street, and then he saw the lights of a taxi come out of the darkness.

He flagged the cab down.

"The Battery. As fast as you can make it," he said and slammed the door shut.

"Okay."

"The nine o'clock ferry. There's a sawbuck if you can do it."

"I'll do it."

The cab raced along through the pouring rain, and all the time Brian's mind went back to the gypsy's words.

The bombs are in the timetable.

Brian put on the dome lights and studied the schedule again.

The bombs are in the. . . .

And then he saw what Jo-Jo had meant.

"They are," he whispered to himself. "They sure are."

Down in the fine print of the schedule were the words: "Life preservers are in the footlockers under the benches."

Curley had penciled a star at the head of the line.

"Hurry," Brian called out. "We're not making it."

"We will."

They're in the footlockers, Brian thought. The bombs are in the footlockers.

"We'll soon be there."

But when they got close to the terminal they were caught in a traffic jam.

"I'll run for it," Brian shouted.

He paid the driver and jumped out of the cab. The terminal loomed in the night a block away. Brian ran, and as he came to the end of the block, he saw a police car standing at the curb.

He made a split-second decision.

"There are bombs on the nine o'clock ferry," he shouted to the cops.

"What?"

"I tell you there's no time. We've got to stop it from going out."

They stared at him, and then one started to get out

of the car, and it was then that Brian remembered the gypsy's words. Not the police. Not yet.

"Dammit, don't you believe me?"

"Wait a minute."

The policeman put his hand out to grab Brian, but Brian whirled away from him and ran up the ramp that led into the terminal. When he was inside he jumped over the turnstiles and dashed to the ferry doors. They were just about to close.

He ran through them and onto the deck of the ship.

Brian threaded his way through the passengers and then went up the staircase to the upper deck. He heard the blast of the ferry whistle, a loud shattering blast. And then the heavy throb of the engines as the ferry slid away from its slip and out into the bay.

Brian came to the top deck. He ran to the gate that led out to the wheelhouse area. He was about to open it and dash in and up the iron steps when a burly deckhand grabbed him and held him back.

"I must see the captain," Brian said. "Quick."

"What for?"

"Tell him there are bombs on the ship. Hurry."

The man stared at him and then turned and ran up the metal staircase and into the cabin. Brian stood there in the rain, his face taut and white. Then he saw the captain, a tall lean man, come hurrying down to him.

"What's this all about?"

"I tell you there are bombs. Time bombs."

"Where? Where?"

And Brian was about to answer when he was grabbed from behind. It was one of the policemen from the car.

"You've got to believe me," Brian shouted, trying to break loose from his grasp. The other policeman had now come up to them.

"Put the cuffs on him."

"No. Give me a chance. Search the footlockers. Now."

The captain looked hard at Brian and then he said curtly, "Search them. Quick!"

They fanned out, and they began to open the panels of the footlockers, one after the other, quickly and almost frantically.

And Brian saw, with a hopeless feeling, that they were finding nothing but life preservers.

"All right," the policeman said grimly to Brian. "You've had your fun."

"Wait!" the deckhand suddenly called out. "He's right, dammit. The kid's right!"

The captain's face blanched. He turned and ran out onto the deck and then up the steps to his cabin.

There was the sound of bells.

And then his voice was heard, crisp and sharp, over the loudspeaker.

"We have an emergency. We are going to turn and head for the Governors Island slip. It is a matter of three minutes to get there. I want you all to line up in orderly rows at once. There are two policemen on board who will supervise you. As soon as we pull into the slip, I want everybody to leave this ship. I will remain on it with a single member of the crew. I want you to leave this ship quietly, calmly and as quickly as possible. I repeat, as quickly as possible. There is no danger. But leave the ship."

The boat slowly turned and then headed swiftly for the lights of Governors Island. All of the passengers moved forward and stood in silent lines, their faces tight and drawn. But no one spoke a word.

It was an eerie, expectant silence. As if everyone knew that their lives were in balance and that the slightest word would shatter their world to bits.

The boat eased into the slip and the people silently debarked. Brian stood between the two policemen and watched the doomed ship back slowly out into the current.

Suddenly the harbor was crowded with lights of other boats, small and large, sailing into the area. The ferry stopped mid-channel and stood in the driving rain, a large, formless bulk.

A huge searchlight played upon it. And then another one.

Brian saw a helicopter come out from shore and then stop and hover over the ferry. He watched as first one figure and then another was lifted off the ferry.

"That was the captain," the policeman said quietly to Brian. "There's no one on it now."

Then they all stood there, a silent throng, still not a word, all eyes were on the doomed ship.

Then came the explosions, one after the other. The huge mass tilted and then slowly sank into the rainy waters.

"You just saved a lot of lives," the policeman said.

But Brian thought of Aram and of Donna.

I could not save them, he said to himself.

25

They took a walk to the river, and after that he was to leave and go home. The day was warm and soon summer would be coming in. They sat on a bench, silently watching the passing boats and the sun as it lay gently on the water.

It's all over, he thought to himself. Marian has confessed the murder of Donna. Tod and Rolfe are behind bars.

"And so it's about over," he said.

"Yes, Brian."

He picked up a small shining piece of glass from the ground and scaled it over the water. The glass sparkled and sank. He was silent.

"Are you thinking of Donna?" she asked gently.

A haunted look came into his eyes.

"She will always be with me. I'll never be free of her." And then he said slowly, "I don't think I'd ever want to be."

After a while they walked back to her place. They spoke little on the way. They stopped in front of her door.

"I've so much to thank you for," he said.

"Don't," she said softly. "Just let it be."

He looked at her and he saw the changing lights in her hazel eyes, and he wanted to say to her, You are a very beautiful woman, Ellen Fisher.

"Good-bye," he said.

And then he turned and left her.

26

When the bus let him off, the day had turned grey. The sun was high and dim in the sky. He walked the blocks till he came to his own. Then he turned and walked a few steps and saw his mother standing in front of the house.

Standing on the sidewalk.

He raised his hand slowly, and then he saw her tremble and begin to hurry to him. Till he had his arms about her.

"Brian," she said.

And she was weeping.

JAY BENNETT is the only writer to win, in two successive years, The Mystery Writers of America's Award for the "best juvenile mystery." The author of many suspense novels for young adults, Mr. Bennett has also written successful adult novels, stage plays, and radio and television scripts.

Mr. Bennett's professed aim in his young adult novels (that have sold over a million copies) is "to write honest books that speak about violent times . . . but throughout the books, and in every word I write, there is a cry against violence."

Novels for Young Adults From Avon Flare

BREAKING UP
by Norma Klein   55830...$1.95

In this novel by the award-winning author of SUNSHINE and MOM, THE WOLF MAN AND ME, a 15-year-old finds that difficult decisions are an important part of growing up, as she is forced to make choices in the custody battle between her divorced parents, and between her possessive best friend and a new love. FLARE NOVEL.

MARIANA
by Karen Strickler Dean   78345...$1.95

Ms. Dean, a former dancer, and author of Avon's MAGGIE ADAMS, DANCER, conveys the excitement and discipline of the dance world to her readers. 15-year-old Mariana finds herself torn between two dreams when she falls in love for the first time—and risks undoing all her years of rigorous ballet training. FLARE ORIGINAL NOVEL.

THE PIGEON
by Jay Bennett   55348...$1.95

From the author of Avon's THE KILLING TREE, a brilliantly suspenseful story of a teenage boy who's been set up for his girlfriend's murder. "Bennett's latest thriller measures up to works that have twice won him Edgars . . . The fast, twisty story is hugely entertaining."
                    —*Publishers Weekly*. FLARE MYSTERY.